The Billion

Billionaire B.

Penelope Ryan

Alec: I've made a stupid mistake, and now pretending that she's my wife is the only way to seal the biggest business deal of my life. She's young, witty, and irritating—but I can't deny she's sexy as hell.

Ella: He's always been nothing but the asshole billionaire I dog-walk for. That is, until he needs a massive favor, and I'm the only one who can help. A week on a Caribbean cruise with the hottest older man I've ever known, pretending to be his wife? What could go wrong?

Alec King, the oldest brother and co-founder of King Technologies, is about to close the biggest deal of his life. The only problem? The man who holds all the power in his hands only wants to do business with married, traditional, "family" men. In a moment of panic, Alec lies, and when his dog-walker comes in, his dog in tow, he impulsively introduces her as his wife.

While recent college grad and dog-walker Ella Reed may like his dog, she most certainly doesn't like Alec King. With never a kind word to share, and always a concescending frown, she dreads their run-ins. So when he comes to her with a proposition that includes spending an entire week together, pretending to be married and in love, she initially says no.

But Alec is persistent. And not only that, he's offering her money—enough money to pay for her dream vet school she's been saving up for.

Against both of their better judgements, Alec and Ella embark on a Caribbean cruise with Alec's brothers and their potential new business partner. But pretending to be in love can blur the lines, and when an angry fight somehow turns into a night of pure bliss, it has both of them wondering how fake this relationship is.

But Alec is hesitant to love again, and Ella is worried she'll never live up to the standards of a billionaire's wife. And as their relationship tumbles even further into the unknown, can they unravel it without breaking their hearts?

3

This story is a work of fiction. Any references to real events, people, or places are used fictitiously. Other names, events, characters, or places are a product of the author's imagination and any resemblance to actual names, events, people, or places is completely coincidental.

Copyright 2024 by Penelope Ryan

Chapter 1

Ella

I pull my coat tight around me, bracing myself for the frigid, Seattle cold as I step out the front door of my apartment complex and jog down the steps to the sidewalk. A gust of wind blows through my hair, and I grit my teeth at the chill. Frigid is right.

Well, maybe not frigid as in icy, but definitely frigid as in *wet*. Seattle has wet winters, which, arguably, are much, much worse. A light drizzle permeates the air, and I can feel my hair frizzing already. It's the main reason I never bother to style it. What's the use?

I check the time on my phone. 9:17. Exactly thirteen minutes to get to Alec King's penthouse.

Because only Alec King would care that I be *exactly* on time to walk his dog. I roll my eyes just thinking about him.

When I first started my dog walking business a year ago, I imagined working for sweet, little, old ladies or fellow college kids, spending time with their adorable pets while they were out of town or otherwise disposed. And, to be fair, I do have quite a few of those types of clients.

But I don't know what the deal is with Alec King. I'd been referred to him by someone else in his apartment complex who I occasionally dog sit for. Apparently, it had been high praise. First, I'd been absolutely dumbfounded by the size of his apartment. No, penthouse. It's a penthouse. I'd never seen one in person before until I started working for him. I'm still shocked that people live like that. Stunning, ridiculous views of Seattle. And besides that, he's just … weird. I don't think I've seen the man smile once. Not once. Not even at his dog. Which is an adorable little Corgi, by the way. How do you not continuously smile at a Corgi? Your *own* Corgi?

Whatever. The point is that Alec King is weird. And kind of an asshole. And gets angry if I'm any more than thirty seconds late to walking that aforementioned Corgi. So here I am hustling through the rainy streets of Seattle on my way to his penthouse. Thankfully, I don't live far from his building. (Only in a much, much less nice area and in a much, much less nice apartment.)

I round the corner toward Alec King's building and see it come into view. I glance around, hoping the drizzle will let up soon so my walk with Betty—the Corgi—isn't absolutely miserable.

I'm still in a little bit of shock that I've managed to make an entire job out of this. I giggle to myself just thinking about it. But I need to remember the bigger picture, my long-term plan—not that it's hard to forget. It's been my dream since I was a teenager.

I just graduated from the University of Washington eight months ago with a degree in Animal Sciences. I'd been lucky enough to have parents who'd saved a college fund for me, making my education practically free on my part. But now, the expensive part comes in. Vet school. It's my ultimate dream, and my calling. The only problem is that vet school is expensive. And sure, I could take out loans—and I probably will—but I also need a good savings net just to live on since going to school full time will make working a bit less feasible. So I'm taking some time to save as much money as humanly possible before I continue on with my dreams of becoming a vet, opening a clinic, and spending each and every day helping animals and the people who love them. I get excited just thinking about it.

I walk through the front doors of Alec King's apartment building, and the apartment manager smiles at me from the front desk. I wave. As the dog walker for Alec King, as well as another tenant in the building, he's used to me by now.

I swipe the keycard Alec has given me to gain access to the penthouse floor, and I step into the elevator. Once on the top floor, I make my way down the hall. There are a few penthouses up here, and Alec's is the one at the end of the hall. I stop in front of the door, fiddling with my keys in my purse, searching for the right one.

But just as I'm pulling it free, the door swings open. I look up, startled.

"Ella." Alec King is standing in the doorway, his jaw tight and his suit pressed almost too nicely. Can he even sit in that thing? His dark hair is perfectly groomed, a small smattering of gray beginning to peak out at his sideburns. I'd clock him in his mid- to late-thirties, although that frown on his face is only going to start wrinkling if he isn't careful. He surveys me with a gaze I can only describe as distasteful before stepping aside, allowing me in.

I frown slightly. "What are you doing home?" I manage to ask after a few heartbeats. He's not normally here during the day—hence why I'm employed to walk Betty. Which is honestly great—the less I have to see him, the better. Our encounters are always awkward and … tense.

He shuts the door behind me, then spins around and heads down a hallway to the left. "I have an important meeting. It's at my brother's, so I've been working here all morning," he calls over his shoulder.

"Your brother's?" I echo, not really expecting him to hear. I vaguely remember him telling me something about working with his brother. Or brothers, if I recall correctly. I can't quite remember what he does. Some tech company stuff—I don't know. A Seattle finance bro, perhaps?

"Yes, he lives next door," Alec says, entering the living room again and setting a briefcase on the kitchen counter.

I nod. So his brother lives next door. In an equally nice penthouse, I assume.

It's now that Betty decides to come waddling into the room, her nails clicking against the hardwood. "Hi, Betty," I say with a smile, bending over to give her a few scratches behind her ears. She wags her tail furiously—or should I say her butt?—and grins up at me.

"Well, good luck with the meeting," I say as I leash up Betty.

He grunts in response without so much as throwing a glance my way.

I roll my eyes, turning so he can't see me.

"Oh, and Ella," he says, pulling my attention back to him. "Make sure you're actually *walking* her. I've noticed Betty getting … pudgy. I pay you to exercise her, not take her to a park and sit."

"Uh …" I stutter. "I mean, I'm definitely walking her—" I defend myself, but he simply waves off my reply.

"Go, I have a lot to prepare for this meeting." With that, he heads back down his hallway, leaving me and Betty alone in the entryway.

Still a bit stunned, I leave the penthouse, Betty on my heels. I stand in the elevator, fuming. "Asshole," I mutter, shaking my head. "And for the record, Betty, you're perfect—pudgy or not."

Chapter 2

Alec

I straighten my tie as I walk down the hall toward Asher's penthouse apartment. I grip the briefcase tightly in my hand, pausing to take a deep breath in front of Asher's door.

My two brothers and I all own penthouses in the same luxury apartment complex in downtown Seattle. They were investments we made right after our company, King Tech, really took off. And while we don't often take business meetings at our homes—after all, we pay quite a bit for a nice office space downtown—this meeting is a little bit different.

I open the door to Asher's place, and I see both my brothers chatting in the dining area as I walk in. Aiden is the first to look up and greet me.

"Hey, Alec," he says.

Asher is busy going through something on his laptop and sends me a quick wave without looking up.

"Ready for the *big meeting*?" Aiden asks me, widening his eyes and grinning.

I resist the urge to roll my eyes at him. As the youngest, Aiden's always been one to tease Asher and I about being overly nervous, worried, and "uptight," as he calls it. Well, if "uptight" is what lands you one of the highest grossing companies in the country and a luxurious penthouse in one of the most expensive places in the city, I'll take it.

"How's the presentation?" I ask Asher. It's what I assume he's presently working on.

Asher nods. "Good. I've gone over it a hundred time the last few days. It better be good."

I open my briefcase and pull out my laptop. I make sure all the necessary files are in place, along with an empty document for notes. Aiden, as usual, seems cool as a cucumber without a care in the world. I don't even think he brought his laptop. Or a fucking notepad.

To the potentially biggest meeting of our lives.

I still can't believe it. King Tech is considering a merger. I never in a million years thought that we'd be in this position. But we grew so quickly in the virtual reality space, that huge companies have started taking notice. And while we definitely don't need outside help—we're doing fine on our own—we were recently presented with an idea that we had to at least consider.

Caddelle Enterprises. The biggest name in VR. The founder had reached out to Asher personally. King Tech specializes in a slightly different form of VR. Rather than entertainment or online spaces, King Tech does more in terms of practical application. We help create programs for doctors, nurses, scientists, and the like to practice skills in a virtual setting before branching out into the real world. It's been revolutionary in the training of thousands of professionals across a myriad of fields.

And Marcus Caddelle wants to join forces. And not just a buyout. A legitimate merger. He wants Caddelle Enterprises and King Tech to become one. Which means billions of dollars more in funding, innovation, as well as profit. It's the opportunity of a lifetime.

And it's about to walk through that door any minute.

"I cannot believe you're so calm," I mutter in Aiden's direction. He merely shrugs.

"We've got this, Alec," Asher says, finally looking up from his laptop. He shoots me an encouraging smile.

We spend the next few minutes readying the presentation, pulling up the first slide on the large TV screen above Asher's dining room table. When a knock sounds at the front door, a flurry of nerves jolts through me.

Asher goes to answer it and in steps Marcus Caddelle. He looks to be in his mid- to late-fifties, with gray hair combed back and black glasses adorning his face. He's slim, wearing a well-fitting gray suit. The first thing I notice about him is his infectious smile.

"Hello, gentlemen," he says as he enters the dining room, reaching out to each of us to enthusiastically shake our hands. "It's so wonderful to finally meet you all in person."

"The pleasure is ours," I assure him. "We're honored to discuss a possible merger with you."

"Would you like something to drink, Marcus?" Asher asks. "Coffee, tea, water?"

"A coffee would be perfect."

Asher steps into the kitchen to pour Marcus a cup. The penthouse is open concept though, so we're all able to continue chatting. Marcus mentions the flight over, his hotel stay, and comments on the beauty of

Seattle. He's never visited before. Aiden is quick to offer his advice on tourist attractions, and after a few minutes, I find myself relaxing. The mood is light, easy, comfortable. As if we're simply catching up with an old friend. I'd already decided that I liked Marcus's company, but now I know that I like Marcus himself. This merger—if it truly goes through—might end up better than I ever thought.

After a few minutes sipping on coffee, we jump into the presentation. Asher goes through the slides we'd painstakingly spent the last few weeks on, pointing out King Tech's strengths, as well as our ideas for merging companies, what we think could be improved, as well as our questions for Marcus and his thoughts.

True to his personality, Marcus chimes in and answers our questions happily and comfortably. We all end up agreeing on most things. And by the time our meeting is coming to a close, a giddiness is starting to spread through me. Because I think this is actually happening. This is actually going to happen.

"I'm feeling good about this," Asher says, glancing to each of us to gauge our reactions.

I grin. "This meeting has gone incredibly," I agree. "I honestly couldn't imagine a better partnership."

Marcus is nodding along. "I like you boys. I hoped I would, based on your work and our brief email exchanges, but now it's been proven." He smiles, leaning back in his seat and taking a sip of coffee. "And I have to say," he adds. "I appreciate business partners who are down to earth, who prioritize the *real*, important things in life." There's a beat of quizzical silence before Marcus points to the framed photo on the wall behind Asher.

Asher turns, and his face lights up both in realization and in happiness. The photo is of him and his wife, Olivia, on their wedding day.

Marcus then gestures to Aiden's left hand where a gold band sits on his ring finger. He and his wife, Lilly, were married almost a year ago. "It's so rare to see these days—especially in the tech world. So many young men with these large, successful companies choose to spend that wealth not on finding a loving wife or starting a family, but instead on extravagance and frankly just playing around." He shakes his head. "It's such a waste. And such a shame."

"She's the one I do it all for," Asher says with a smile.

"As it should be," Marcus approves. "How long have you and your wife been together?"

"Three years now," Asher answers. "And she actually works with us at King Tech. She manages the entire administrative side of things." Asher then grins at Aiden beside him. "And this guy here is technically still a newlywed."

Marcus's smile widens. "Congratulations to you," he says warmly.

Aiden reddens slightly. "Thank you."

Marcus sighs contentedly. "This is such a weight off my chest. The idea of going into business with three family men like yourselves, it really just cements my thoughts on all of this."

"We're so excited to see where this goes," I agree, hoping he won't suddenly notice my lack of wedding band and change his mind on how excited he seems. Besides, it's not like I'm decidedly *not* a "family man." I've just never gotten around to it. Or rather, the one woman I was ready to "get around to it" with was less than thrilled about reciprocating that notion.

But, whatever. That doesn't matter. Not now.

I notice a glint in Marcus's eye, and he leans forward, setting his coffee cup down on the table. "You know, I just had the greatest idea. My wife and I are planning a Caribbean cruise in just a week—why don't the three of you and your wives come along? Our yacht is more than big enough. You can meet my Julia, and it'll be a wonderful chance for all of us to become better acquainted and celebrate this new company we'll be building."

"I'm in," Aiden immediately says. "You had me at 'Caribbean cruise.'"

Asher laughs, scrambling to agree while seeming slightly shocked. "We … could probably find the time to pull ourselves away. This is, after all, our biggest priority at the moment." He gestures to the meeting, insinuating our pending merger.

Marcus clasps his hands together. "Wonderful. This will be such a fun time." Just then, his gaze lands on me. And just as I'd dreaded, it slides down to my ringless left hand. "How rude of me, I never asked about your wife," he says with a hesitant smile. "I assume you're married also?"

I resist the urge to show my cards. To panic and let him know. I can tell he's assessing me. The oldest brother, the one with slightly graying hair, in his late thirties, with no ring on his finger. Fuck. This whole meeting has gone so amazingly well. Could my singleness suddenly ruin everything?

No. No, I can't let us lose this because of me. Because of something as trivial as *not having a wife*. What is this, a fifteenth-century royal treaty?

"Oh, of course," I find myself saying, regretting the words as soon as they slip past my lips. And yet, they keep coming. "My ring is currently being resized." I gently touch my ring finger in explanation.

Understanding and a slight bit of relief wash over Marcus's features. "Ah yes, those pesky things can be rather unforgiving." He chuckles.

I laugh along. "But yes, my wife would gladly join us on your yacht. It's so wonderfully generous of you to invite us."

Aiden is staring me down across the table, but I avoid eye contact. Asher seems a bit stiffer than normal, also eyeing me from the side. But it's too late now. The lie has already slipped out, and there's no going back.

"I'll have my secretary send you all the details. We can continue with the merger process in the meantime, and the next time we discuss further details, we can be sitting out in the Caribbean sun with a cool drink." Marcus smiles, standing.

The four of us head to the door. Asher opens it, and we step out into the hallway.

"The Space Needle is touristy," Aiden is saying as we venture down the hall, "but it's a Seattle staple. You have to do it while you're in town."

Suddenly, a familiar yip catches my attention, and I look up to see Ella and Betty turning the corner. Ella sees us, shoots me a brief smile—well, more like a tight-lipped expression of acknowledgement—and pulls Betty along. But Betty, ever the friendly and excited pup, barrels her way toward me, through the legs of Aiden, Asher, and Marcus, and jumps up on me, barely meeting my knees.

Marcus laughs in surprise, looking down. "Is this your dog?" he asks.

"Yes," I admit, trying to push Betty away.

Ella runs into the fray, grabbing Betty's leash that had been previously yanked out of her hands, and trying to pull her away. "Sorry," she says, and she truly looks like she means it. She looks mortified.

Marcus turns to her. "Not a problem at all, dear." Then his eyes widen slightly. "Oh Alec, is this your wife?"

Panic surges through me, twisting my intestines. Ella's eyes are widening, and she's beginning to shake her head, but I beat her to it. "Yes," I say, wrapping my arm around her petite shoulders and pulling her against me. She's stiff as a board. "This is Ella. Ella, this is Marcus Caddelle, the owner of Caddelle Enterprises."

Marcus holds out his hand. "Pleasure to meet you."

Ella looks utterly shell shocked and confused, and I can only hope that she keeps her mouth shut long enough for me to get us all out of this.

"Hi," she says timidly, shaking his hand. "I'm not sure—"

"Go on inside with Betty, sweetheart," I interrupt her. "I'm just going to show Marcus out." I gently push her toward the door, and thankfully she goes, a look of utter bewilderment on her face.

24

Luckily, Marcus seems oblivious to everyone's discomfort. Not just mine and Ella's, but also Asher and Aiden's. They're both standing as still as statues, their eyes wide in horrified confusion as they watch me continuously dig this hole deeper and deeper.

Fuck. What have I done?

But I don't have the time to mull it over now.

The four of us step into the elevator and head down to the lobby. We walk Marcus out to his car, say our goodbyes, and express our excitement for seeing him again soon. As his car pulls away, the three of us stand in the Seattle drizzle, watching it disappear down the street.

Aiden turns to me pointedly, and I feel dread worming its way through my veins. "What the fuck, man?"

Chapter 3

Alec

What the fuck is right. He's absolutely right.

"Yeah, Alec. Um, what was that?" Asher says quietly.

The drizzle is starting to accumulate on my suit jacket, and I can feel it soaking into my hair. But I can't quite make myself move. Not just yet.

"Alec." Aiden shakes me.

"Okay, yeah," I say, taking a step back and heading into the lobby. My brothers follow me, Aiden a little more insistently than Asher.

"What do you mean, 'yeah, okay'?" Aiden asks. "A wife? You have a wife? Where? Your *dog walker*?"

I'm speed-walking to the elevator, but Aiden and Asher are keeping pace. "I don't know what happened, okay? I was afraid he'd pull the deal if he knew I wasn't married. He seemed so enamored with the fact that you two are such *family men*, and then he assumed I was one too. What was I supposed to do?" I hit the button on the elevator, and the doors close.

"Not make up a fake wife, that's what," Aiden answers.

Asher simply shakes his head.

"I'll deal with it," I assure them.

"Please do," Asher breathes, running his hands over his face. "This is the biggest thing that's ever happened to our company, and I'd rather not blow it over something this … *weird*."

"I know that, okay?" I snap back just as the elevator doors open. I step out into the hallway and beeline toward my apartment, leaving Aiden and Asher alone to no doubt discuss my embarrassing and ridiculous predicament.

I enter my apartment, relieved to be free of my brothers' scrutiny, but now I'm faced with an even bigger problem.

Ella.

She straightens from where she had been leaning against the kitchen counter, Betty snoozing on the floor at her feet. Her frizzy dark hair frames her face—a face that is currently scrunched up in disbelief.

"Uh, so are you going to tell me what *that* was?" she demands, placing her hands on her hips. She can't be much taller than five feet, so her attempt at an intimidating pose isn't exactly working. Although I am nervous. Not so much because of her but because of this idiotic hole I'm continuing to dig for myself.

I close my eyes, taking a deep breath. "Okay. This is going to sound crazy, but I have a favor to ask of you." I open my eyes to see that hers have narrowed.

"A favor," she states.

I nod.

"Does this favor have anything to do with the fact that you told three men out there that I'm your *wife*?" She crosses her arms across her chest.

"You guessed it," I say with a humorless chuckle, although it doesn't quite get the reaction I'm hoping for.

She shakes her head. "Look, I don't know what weird game you're playing, or why you need someone to pretend to be your wife, but you can find someone else to do it." She grabs her purse off the counter and stalks past me toward the door.

I spin after her. "But that's the problem—it has to be you. I already told Marcus Caddelle you're my wife."

"I don't know who that is, and I don't care."

"He owns the business my company is trying to merge with," I say, hoping the severity of the situation will sink in for her.

She shrugs. "And who's problem is that?" she snaps, opening my front door. I have half a mind to slam it shut and demand that she stay and talk with me. But I can't risk actually scaring her off. I *need* her to agree to this.

"Oh, it's definitely my problem, I admit that," I say, rushing after her into the hall. "But I'd pay you. I just need to you pose as my wife. It can't be that hard."

She turns to face me, pursing her lips. "I don't know, Mr. King. You barely trust me to *walk* your dog—worried I spent too much time sitting around in parks."

I can feel myself flushing at her recall of my earlier comment. Fuck.

The elevator arrives, and she steps inside. "I doubt I could handle the complexity of this new offer," she says with an eye roll. And with that, the elevator doors close.

Chapter 4

Ella

The door to my apartment closes behind me, and I stand in the dark entryway for a moment, stunned. Because what the actual hell?

The soft padding of paws against the hardwood has me turning to see Howard, my golden retriever, loping up to me. He wags his tail, nuzzling against my thigh.

"Hey there, Howie," I say, reaching down to pat him on the head.

I walk into my living room—or should I say the entirety of my apartment? I do have a separate bedroom and bathroom, but my living room and kitchen are smushed into an area barely big enough for a couch and a TV.

I toss my purse on the couch and sit down beside it.

Did Alec King really just propose what I think he did? I blink a few times, rubbing my eyes. I'd laugh out loud at the absurdity if I wasn't pretty sure that I'd just lost one of my highest paying dog walking gigs. He's definitely not going to want me around anymore. I bite my lip, wondering if I should have held in my anger back there.

But honestly, he'd deserved it. He's been nothing but an asshole to me the entire time I've worked for him. I've known him for a year, and he's never once even smiled at me. Asked how my day was going, said a kind word at all. The only time he goes out of his way to talk to me is to criticize something—like this morning when he'd insinuated that I didn't *walk* Betty enough. Like, what the hell, man?

And then, barely an hour later, he turns around and asks the most ridiculous favor in the entire universe? No. That's not how this works. Alec King is a man who's used to bossing people around and getting whatever he wants, I'm sure. But I want nothing to do with it. Especially pretending to be his wife? God, what an awful gig that would be.

I check the time on my phone. Normally I have just one other dog walking gig today—an older lady who just can't quite exercise her Labrador retriever as much as he needs. But her son is visiting from out of town today, so she doesn't need the help.

Which means the rest of my day is wide open.

I grab my laptop, pulling up my internet browser. There's already some searches still up. The best veterinary schools in the Seattle area. I'm pretty sure I've narrowed it down and know where I want to go. The only issue now is saving the money and applying for loans. It's overwhelming to think about, but I really need to get on it.

It's been over half a year since I graduated. I'd planned on taking a gap year to save money, but if I want to start school next fall, I should probably start applying now.

A sudden knock on my door pulls me from my thoughts. I turn to stare at it, unsure it was even an actual knock. Maybe one of the neighbors simply dropped something out in the hallway. But a few seconds later, the knock comes again, louder and more persistent this time.

I frown, standing. Who would be knocking at my door? My family and friends rarely come over unannounced. I check my phone to see if I have any unnoticed texts. Nope.

I walk up to the door and hesitantly glance through the peephole.

No way.

I yank the door open to see none other than Alec King standing in the doorway of my shitty apartment complex. He looks as out of place as one could possibly be. That overly pressed suit, those shiny dress shoes, and ... a bouquet of flowers?

He levels me with a cool stare. "Can we talk?"

I glance between him and the flowers in confusion. "I … how did you know I live here?"

"It was on your application when I hired you."

Oh yeah. He'd been the only one to have me fill out a formal application before hiring me to walk his dog. Like I was taking a job at his company. It reeked of pretention, and it definitely still does.

"Can we talk?" he repeats.

I stare at him for a heartbeat more. "I guess." I step aside. My entryway is narrow, so he has to practically brush against me to get into the living space. I've never been this close to him. God, he's tall. And he smells like … pine? Or is that the flowers?

But then he's passed me and is standing awkwardly in my living room, glancing around. I close the door and follow him in. Howard hurries up to him, sniffing and wagging his tail. Alec stiffens awkwardly.

I stand a few feet away, shuffling my feet and crossing my arms. "I assume you wanna talk more about the wife thing, yeah?"

His expression doesn't change. He simply assesses me with that calculating look he always wears. God, does this guy even have feelings? Is he a goddamn robot?

"Yes," he answers. "I realize it was completely unfair of me to spring it on you the way I did, but I'd like a chance to explain the situation and give you my offer."

My offer. Like this is some kind of business deal. Which, I guess, it probably is. I vaguely remember him offering to pay me something before I'd stormed out by how weird that entire encounter had been.

I'm torn between throwing him out and actually hearing what he has to say. At the very least, it's got to be entertaining. And I have to admit I am a bit curious as to why he'd randomly pulled me over and introduced me as his wife.

"Okay, sure. I'll hear your offer."

He nods. Then he glances around. "Do you have a vase for these?" He holds out the flowers.

So I guess they *are* for me. I purse my lips. "I have a cup."

He raises his eyebrows. "Would you like to put them in ... *a cup*?"

I shrug, turning around and pulling out a drinking class from a cabinet above the kitchen counter. I fill it with some water and turn back around to take the flowers from Alec's outstretched hand. I put them in the glass and set it on the counter.

Seemingly satisfied, Alec continues. "King Tech has an incredible opportunity with Marcus Caddelle. We're considering merging our companies. In fact, we almost certainly are. There's only one problem. Marcus values business partners with family values—business partners with ..." Alec's expression looks pained, "*wives.*"

I nod. I see. "Okay so this guy wants you to be married. Sure. But you couldn't find someone better to play pretend with? Or at least *ask me* before you introduce me as such?"

Alec's pained expression deepens. "Yeah. I realize how inappropriate that was. I, uh ... honestly, Marcus saw you walking my dog, made an assumption, and I just ... went with it."

I stare at him for a long, long moment. He actually looks ... uncomfortable. Upset, worried, nervous. I've never seen him anything other than aloof and domineering. It's actually kind of fun to see him like this. Watching him squirm.

I lean back against my kitchen countertop with a soft smirk. "So it's me or nothing?"

He lets out a frustrated sigh. "Basically."

I nod again. "Okay."

Alec's eyes widen slightly. "You'll do it?"

"No, I said 'okay,' as in 'okay, I understand,' not 'okay, I'll do it.'"

A flicker of annoyance flutters across his face, stirring some satisfaction within me. "Please, Ella," he says. It's the first time he's really called me by my name other than in his apartment hallway earlier when introducing me. "I'll pay you. *A lot.* This is an opportunity I can't blow. I need this to go smoothly."

But as much as I'm enjoying watching Alec King squirm, I'm starting to grow tired of this game. And just like when he'd first proposed this, I'm doubting what the details of this entail, what this really means. I shake my head, dropping the smirk and getting real. "I don't know. I don't even know what pretending to be your wife would look like. It all sounds … shady, and iffy."

"It'll be easy," Alec presses. "All you have to do is stand beside me and act like we're a couple. Maybe we'll hold hands, but that's the most. We don't even have to kiss if that's something you're not comfortable with. We can just say we don't prefer PDA. It'll be the easiest hundred grand you've ever made."

At his last comment, my eyes widen, and suddenly my attention is fully caught. "I'm sorry, did you say *one hundred grand*?"

It's Alec's turn to smile, and I hate the feeling of him having the upper hand. But he does, and we both know it. "Yes. Like I said, it'll be the easiest hundred grand you've ever made."

I narrow my eyes. "Come on. You're not going to pay me that much just to hang out with you. Platonically. Without …?"

"I swear to god that it will all be above board," he's quick to answer. "Nothing sexual, nothing inappropriate, and nothing you're not comfortable with."

I continue to assess him with my narrowed gaze. My gut is telling me no. That this is a crazy idea, that there's no way we'd be able to pull it off, and that Alec is an asshole anyway, so what do I owe him? The only problem is that hundred grand. My mind keeps getting stuck on it—over and over again. Shit, a hundred grand could change my life. A hundred grand could pay for a decent chunk of vet school. Almost all of it. I could start my career debt free. The idea of that is practically exhilarating.

Noticing my hesitancy, Alec takes a tentative step forward. "It'll be easy. I promise," he presses.

Fuck. I'm trying hard to push away that fantasy of a hundred grand, but it's becoming more and more tangible as the seconds tick by. And I don't think I'll be able to turn it down. God. Am I really going to do this?

"I ... guess," I finally say.

He raises his eyebrows. "Really?"

I shrug. "Sure. Yeah. What the hell?"

The corner of his mouth ticks upward in a smirk. It's the closest thing to a smile I've ever seen from him. Although this one is irritatingly smug. Jesus. How am I supposed to pretend to be this guy's wife when whenever he smiles, I wanna smack him in the face?

"Thank you, Ella. I mean it," he says.

I nod, even though I'm still unconvinced. But whatever my feelings are, we're going for it. I agreed, and here we are.

"Oh, there's one more thing," he adds. "How do you feel about Caribbean vacations?"

Chapter 5

Ella

There were a lot of ways I saw my gap year after college panning out. Growing my dog walking business, saving money for vet school, spending time with friends, maybe making a trip out to California to live out some surfer girl fantasy for a weekend. But becoming a billionaire's wife and spending a week on a million-dollar yacht in the Caribbean surely was not one of them.

Well, *fake* wife. But in a way, that's even more insane.

Who hires a girl to be their fake wife? Before Alec had left my apartment yesterday, he'd briefly told me about Marcus Caddelle and the company merger. I guess I get it. But then again, why not just tell the truth? Is this Marcus guy some sort of asshole? Some intimidating jerk Alec and his brothers were worried about offending? It's hard to imagine Alec being intimidated by anyone. But I suppose we all have our breaking points.

And now I have to spend a week in the company of this weird guy—along with Alec's brothers and their wives? Ugh. I can only assume they're all as pretentious and irritating as Alec himself.

A knock at my door pulls me from my thoughts. I set down my cup of tea I'd been nursing and head to the door. I open it to find a delivery man with a rather large box that he's plopped down at my doorstep.

"Ella Reed?" he asks politely.

"Yes," I say eyeing the box suspiciously.

"Sign here." He holds out one of those digital pads. I sign it quickly, and he smiles and bids me a good day, then wanders off.

I stare at the box before me. It's big. Way too big to have been something I ordered. Sure, I've been known to online shop. I'm a sucker for skincare sales, and I love a fun shoe. But this definitely isn't something I bought.

I reach down and awkwardly slide it into my apartment. Once it's in the living room, I grab a pair of scissors from the counter and open it up. Within the box are lots of smaller boxes and bags, with a note on top. I reach for it.

For the trip, it reads. Signed simply, *Alec*.

Ah. I should have guessed this was from him. But what *is* it? I toss the note aside and curiously explore the box. Almost immediately, I notice a box with a name I recognize. My eyes widen. Holy shit.

Chanel.

I reach for it, opening it gingerly to find three dresses inside, all roughly knee-length and warm weather appropriate. I notice a price tag still attached to one, and I immediately check it out. My mouth nearly drops to the floor. What the actual hell?

I continue perusing the box, finding sandals, shorts, tops, and some swimsuits, along with a purse and sunglasses—all from ridiculously nice brands. I'm torn between utter elation at the finery before me and a twinge of irritation. Did Alec assume *my own* things wouldn't be nice enough to display to his brothers and future business partner?

Sure, I don't own a Chanel swimsuit, but who would even notice?

Just then, I notice another smaller box at the bottom the large box. I reach for it, opening it up to find what looks to be a diamond ring inside. My eyes widen at the size of it. Holy shit. Is this *real*?

I slide it onto my left ring finger and stare down at it. Oof. A weird feeling flutters through my stomach.

Once again, it hits me what I've agreed to. Alec had said we'd go into more detail about it over the coming days, and that the trip would begin next week.

I suddenly feel overwhelmed staring at the box of clothes I'm supposedly going to be wearing on a yacht in the Caribbean next week.

I glance at the time on my phone. 5:30 p.m. It's after working hours, so presumably Alec would be home by now, right?

I grab my coat from a hook in the entryway, grab my keys, and head out the door. It's a quick walk to Alec's building, and soon I'm at his door, knocking.

I wait a few seconds, to silence. Technically, I have keys to his place. It's how I get in to walk Betty. But it feels inappropriate to use them now. I knock again, but after a few minutes, I resign myself to the fact that he's probably not home.

I should have guessed this. He's most definitely the workaholic type. He probably works late into the night.

I sigh in annoyance. I pull out my phone and pull up Alec's number. I've had it since I started working for him, although I've never had a reason to call it. After a moment of hesitancy, I call the number.

He picks up after a few rings.

"Ella?"

"Yeah," I answer. "Uh. Are you home?"

There's a shuffling sound on the other end of the line. "Almost."

Suddenly the elevator dings from behind me, and I turn to see Alec King standing inside, his cell pressed to his ear. He purses his lips when he sees me, ending the call and putting his phone away.

"Do you need something?" he asks, brushing past me to unlock his door. He steps inside, beckoning me to follow.

"Yeah, actually," I say, stepping inside his apartment. "I got that box you sent me."

He nods. "Good. Do the clothes fit? I had my secretary guess your size."

48

I frown. I've never even met his secretary. Did he show them a picture of me?

"I don't ... actually know yet," I admit. "I haven't tried them on. But—why did you send them to me in the first place?" I ask, shaking my head.

He frowns. "So you have things to wear on the cruise."

I raise my eyebrows, my hands settling on my hips. "Oh, so you assumed I wouldn't have anything of my own to wear?"

"Yes."

I blink, taken aback by the simplicity of his statement. "You think I don't own swimsuits?" I fire back at him. "Or a dress?"

He sighs. "You're not going on this vacation as Ella Reed, you're going on this vacation as Ella *King*, my *wife*."

My name attached to his sends an odd fluttering feeling through my stomach, but I try to ignore it. "And?" I press.

At this, he looks annoyed. "And no wife of mine would be dressed in anything less than the best."

"Hm." I can feel the anger churning inside me. "So you just assumed, without even asking or taking a look for yourself, that anything I own wouldn't be 'the best'?"

He stares at me for a long moment, taking in my tone, the expression on my face. He cocks an eyebrow. "I know what I pay you, and I can therefore extrapolate your income. And no, I doubt that income can buy you that box I just sent over."

An angry flush creeps up my cheeks. Did he really just say that? If he's trying to rid himself of the asshole persona like he seemed to be doing yesterday, he's failing horribly.

I sigh angrily. "Fine."

"You're welcome for the clothing, by the way," he says.

At this, I can't take it anymore. "No," I snap back. "*You're welcome* that I agreed to this crazy scheme."

My response seems to throw him for a moment, but he quickly regains his composure. "You're right, I suppose," he finally says, although the words sound like glass coming out of his mouth.

I nod curtly, internally satisfied by his admission. But just then, another thought comes to mind. Something that hadn't even crossed my mind in the whirlwind of the last twenty-four hours.

"Who's going to watch Betty when we're away?" My eyes widen. "Or Howard?"

Alec's eyebrow quirks upward. "Howard?"

"My dog. The golden retriever you met yesterday."

He nods. "Ah. Yes. I was planning on hiring a service to take care of Betty while we're away, as well as all your other dog walking clients. I'll add *Howard* to the list. Just let me know your dog walking schedule and I'll pass it along."

Oh. Well, I guess he's thought of everything. "That sounds ... good," I manage.

After a few beats of awkward silence, Alec adds, "If you haven't had dinner yet, you're more than welcome to stay. We can order in and discuss more of the details of our arrangement. It's something we'll have to do sooner or later anyway."

Way to really sell the night. But he's right. And we might as well spend a bit of time together before going off on the trip. After all, we do have to pretend that we're married. We need to at least seem comfortable around each other.

I nod. "Sure. Why not?"

Alec pulls out his phone to order us dinner, and I reach down to pet Betty, still in complete and utter shock as to what I've agreed to do.

Chapter 6

Alec

"I can't believe you're actually going through with this," Aiden declares.

I zip up my suitcase and turn to face him. He's standing in the doorway of my bedroom, an exasperated—yet amused—expression on his face. "Well, considering I'm about to go pick her up in a few minutes, you should probably believe it," I answer.

"You're really paying a girl to pretend to be your wife for the weekend." He trails after me into the kitchen where I pour myself some coffee in a travel mug. It's a statement, but it's still posed as a question.

I sigh in frustration. "What else should I do, Aiden?" I ask. "Go back to Marcus and say, 'Yeah, remember that wife I introduced you to? Turns out that was all fake, and she's actually just my dog walker.' That'll go over well."

Aiden purses his lips. "Asher's really stressed about this, you know," he finally replies.

"Asher's always stressed about everything."

Aiden snorts.

I hold up the coffee pot in offering, but Aiden shakes his head. "But your dog walker?" he asks with a raised eyebrow.

"Ella's her name," I'm quick to add.

"Isn't she a bit young? I mean, is Marcus going to buy that?"

"He did the other day."

"Yeah, but once he meets her. I mean, she's a *lot* younger than you."

I bristle, shooting him a look. Although, I suppose he's right. Now that I think about it, I don't actually know how old Ella is. I know she's out of college. But only recently. Which would make her … *young.* At thirty-seven, I know I'm not exactly a spring chicken, but age gaps aren't that unusual. "It'll be fine," I snap at Aiden.

He rolls his eyes.

"You're going to be ready to head out soon?" I ask Aiden, eyeing him up and down and wondering why he isn't in his own apartment packing a bag. We're all flying down to Florida today. Asher, Aiden, Olivia, Lilly, and Ella and I. And while the jet is owned by us and we technically can't "miss our flight," I don't want to be delayed by someone dragging their feet—which Aiden is known to do.

"Yep, packed last night."

I pass him, grabbing my suitcase from my bedroom and rolling it out into the hall. "Well, good. I'm off to pick up Ella. I'll see you all at the jet."

I grab my travel mug from the counter and head to the door, Aiden following me. "And remember, stick with the story, and please be nice to her. She's already grumpy enough about having to do this," I mutter.

Aiden quirks an eyebrow at my last comment, but lets it be. "Of course we'll be nice to her," he says with a wave.

I head to the elevator, taking it to the garage floor and trekking over to my car. I throw my suitcase in the trunk, get in, and pull out of the garage.

It only takes me five minutes to get to Ella's place. I park on the street and jog up the front steps, down the corridor, and knock on her apartment door. After a few seconds, I hear the latch, and the door opens.

She smiles hesitantly at me, turning to grab her suitcase from behind her. She leans down to her dog— Howard, is it?—giving him a few pats and kisses and mumbling something unintelligible to him. Then she follows me out the door, closing and locking it behind her.

"You wearing the ring?" I ask, making sure the most important apparel I'd sent her is currently sitting on her finger.

She waves her hand in front of me in confirmation. The diamond glistens in the early morning light. I'm wearing a matching gold band on my own left ring finger. It feels strange and … heavy.

Ella's hair is up in a messy bun, and she's wearing leggings and a baggy sweatshirt. She'll definitely have to change before meeting Marcus and his wife, but I can't help but notice just how *cute* she looks.

I stare at her for a few heartbeats before realizing how weird that is and striding forward toward the car in silence. I've never really checked out Ella before. Sure, she's objectively attractive, I know that. But I've never really stopped to consider that attractiveness. And now, early in the morning, her messy hair piled atop her head and her face still a bit puffy from sleep, I'm overcome with the urge to wrap her up in my arms and just hug her.

I slam into my car a bit too hard, popping the trunk, and tossing her suitcase inside. *Shut up, Alec,* I chide myself I'm probably just stressed. Overwhelmed by the enormity of this ruse. This ridiculous ruse that I need to work.

"You packed the stuff I sent you?" I ask as we both get into the car.

"Of course," she answers.

Trying to lighten the mood, I turn to her with a soft smile. "Ready to be my wife for the week?"

She laughs quietly. "Ready as I'll ever be, *hubby*."

Her voice sends a chill down my spine, and I look away quickly. Hubby. *You're a husband now, Alec. For one week. Remember that.*

I put the car into gear and head off toward the airport.

Chapter 7

Ella

We drive for about thirty minutes until we reach a small, private airport on the outskirts of Seattle. The mood in the car is … tense. The last week, we've gotten together a few times to go over our backstory and mainly just hang out a bit so that we're slightly more used to each other and natural.

But I think the nerves are finally getting to us. At least to me. Because today is the day. In just a few minutes, I'll be meeting Alec's brothers and their wives—who know about our lie, obviously, but it's still daunting. And tonight, I'll be meeting Marcus and Julia Caddelle, the people who we really need to fool. The pressure is on. And I think we're both feeling it.

We enter the small airport, and Alec pulls our car into a garage. I take a deep breath as I get out of the car, steeling my already fried nerves.

Alec opens the trunk and pulls out our suitcases, handing me mine.

"Ready to go?" he asks.

I nod. It's not like I can back out now.

I follow him as we exit the garage, and it's then that I see the plane. Even though I knew that we'd be flying privately, it's still impressive to actually see. The private jet sits about fifty feet away with a staircase propped up against the door. We wheel our suitcases up to it, where someone takes our bags, and then Alec starts up the stairs. I follow.

Inside, the jet is both exactly as I expected yet somehow more lavish than I could ever imagine. I've never flown privately—obviously. My flying experiences have been comprised of cramped seats, pushy seat neighbors, and bad coffee. But this? This is insane.

We're immediately met by two long couches against the sides of the plane, facing each other. A TV is mounted against the wall and looks pliable enough to pull out and adjust so all passengers can watch. As the plane continues, there are large, cushiony chairs toward the back—but unlike normal airliners where the chairs are stiff and crammed in, these are luxurious. They twirl, with plenty of ample leg room.

But as much as I'd love to keep ogling the interior of this plane, it's then that I notice four people who I assume are Alec's brothers and their wives. And they've noticed us. Or, more accurately, *me*.

"Guys," Alec calls out as we enter. "This is Ella." He gestures to me. "Ella, this is Asher and his wife, Olivia." Asher waves, and Olivia shoots me a warm smile. She's absolutely gorgeous—probably the most beautiful person I've ever seen. But her smile puts me at ease somewhat. "And this is Aiden and his wife, Lilly." They both smile in return.

"Welcome, Ella," Lilly says. She's curled up on the couch next to Aiden, her hand on his knee. "It's nice to meet you." The others all murmur their agreement, although I can definitely detect a hint of awkwardness in the air. And it's not like I can blame them. This is most definitely the most awkward thing I can imagine. I wonder what they're thinking about Alec's plan. I'd love to get some details from the girls. I wonder if they'd share any insights with me, or if they'd clam up in the hopes of protecting their brother-in-law.

Lilly pats the empty space beside her on the couch, and I take a seat, grateful that they are at least being welcoming, if not a little hesitant.

"Have you ever been to the Caribbean?" she asks.

Alec takes a seat across from me on the other couch next to Asher and Olivia.

I shake my head. "I haven't traveled much," I admit.

Lilly and I continue with our small talk for a bit, Aiden and Olivia chiming in with anecdotes or questions from time to time. I notice Asher and Alec engrossed in a hushed conversation—probably either about the big merger or my and Alec's predicament. Or both.

After a few moments, I feel the engines shutter to life, and soon we're taxiing down the runway. I turn on the couch to look out the window as the plane takes off, reveling in the view of Seattle from the sky. And the fact that I'm looking out the window from a *couch*. I could pinch myself. In fact, I'm still not a hundred percent convinced this whole thing isn't a dream. And it's only about to get dreamier. I mean, we're heading to a yacht off the coast of Florida and will be sailing the Caribbean. It doesn't get much dreamier than that.

A soft touch to my arm grabs my attention, and I turn around. Alec is standing above me. "Want to go over our story a bit more?" he suggestions, gesturing to the back of the plane.

The others are engaged in conversation, so we quietly brush past them to the empty seats at the back of the plane. We're far enough away now that neither of our conversations will be heard by the others.

"You feeling okay about everything?" Alec asks as we sit side by side.

I shrug. "Pretty much. Your family is nice."

At this, I think I see a hint of the first genuine smile I've ever seen from him. "Yeah. They're pretty great." He clears his throat. "Alright. Backstory—what we discussed. Go." He gestures to me.

Nerves dance through my stomach, and I'm suddenly feeling the pressure. He was right to suggest we go over it all again. We have to have this right. We can't mess this up. I nod. "Okay. We met through mutual friends only a year ago. It was a whirlwind romance, love at first sight. We were married barely six months into knowing each other. The relationship is still young, which would explain any potential gaps in our knowledge of each other."

Alec nods.

"We had a small wedding with just family and friends back in July. We're still in the honeymoon phase and just enjoying each other's company, so any questions about future plans, kids, anything, will be met with 'who knows?'"

Alec chuckles. "And don't forget about *our* dog, Betty, who Marcus saw you walking the other day."

I feign offense. "I could never forget about Betty."

He snorts. We sit in a comfortable silence for a few heartbeats, before Alec poses another question. "We should also probably talk about boundaries. And the logistics of those boundaries."

I nod slowly. He's right. I hadn't actually thought much about it, other than his insistence upon our arrangement being "appropriate" when he'd first begged me to agree.

"We can start with sleeping arrangements," Alec says. "I obviously couldn't request separate rooms for us, but I've been told that each suite has a couch. I'll be happy to sleep there while you take the bed, and I'll make a point to give you as much privacy as possible."

I nod. I'd assumed we'd be sharing a room once the entirety of the trip had been presented to me. It's a relief to hear that Alec has already anticipated sleeping on the couch. I was ready to strongarm him into it if needed. Which I am more than certain I'd be capable of doing.

"As for PDA," he continues. "We do have to at least appear comfortable with each other."

"And, according to our backstory, we're still in a bit of a honeymoon phase," I add.

Alec nods slowly, surveying me. Finally, he asks, "What, exactly, are you comfortable with?"

I pause for a moment. I hadn't thought much of it until now, which I realize might have been naïve. And now, on the spot, I'm not sure what to say. "Well ..." I begin slowly. "I suppose anything I'm totally uncomfortable with would be things we'd never do in public anyway."

Alec swallows, and is it just my imagination, or do his cheeks flush with slightly more color?

"So I suppose holding hands, sitting near each other, light physical contact—that's all okay with me," I elaborate.

"And kissing?"

Kissing. Hmm. How *do* I feel about kissing Alec King? It's not like he's unattractive. As a matter of fact, he's not bad looking at all. He's got this rugged quality, a confidence that's borderline sexy. And I've always been somewhat into older men. But something about kissing Alec King feels dangerous. Like a destination I could never return from.

"Let's say that kissing isn't completely off the table," I finally answer. "But we'll only do it if absolutely necessary."

Alec seems to accept this. "Agreed."

We fall into another bout of silence. This one a bit less comfortable. Probably because we're both thinking about kissing each other. Or at least, *I'm* thinking about kissing *him*. What his lips would feel like against my own. If he'd be soft and sweet, or more aggressive and passionate.

I take a breath, trying to calm my racing heart.

"Maybe we should try out … some physical contact," Alec breaks me out of my thoughts by saying.

I look up at him, slightly alarmed.

"You know, my arm around yours, holding hands? Just so we appear more comfortable when we have to do this in front of Marcus and his wife."

"Oh," I reply. "Yeah. That's probably a good idea."

Alec scoots toward me in his seat. The chairs aren't terribly close to one another, but close enough that he can span the gap between us and loop his arm over my shoulders. His hand rests on my upper arm, gripping it softly. I lean into the crook of his body, inhaling the scent of him, feeling his muscular arm wrapping around me.

We're both definitely stiff at first. His feels like a concrete brick. Or is that just muscle? Does Alec work out? *Ella, stop. You're not allowed to think these things.*

Never in my life did I think I'd ever be this close to Alec King. And never in my life did I think I'd actually enjoy it. Because ... am I enjoying this? Being wrapped up against him, feeling safe and secure and ...

Ella!

I sit up, and Alec's arm falls back to his side. "I think that's good for now," I say quickly. "I mean, I think we'll be fine. Don't you?"

He's nodding before I've even finished my sentence. "Yeah. It'll come naturally. I'm not worried about it."

There's another beat of uncomfortable silence. "Want to go back up with the others?" Alec suggests. "So you can get more acquainted with them? After all, we'll have to pretend you know them well too."

I nod. "That's a good idea." I stand before Alec has the chance to, making my way back to the front of the place, trying to rid my mind of the feeling of Alec's arm around me and how badly I want it to happen again.

Chapter 8

Alec

We land in Miami about five hours later to bright sunshine and gorgeous palm trees. Ella's face lights up the second she steps out of the plane and feels the humidity on her skin. She'd changed on the plane and is how wearing a floral, knee-length dress that's modest but still hugs her curves in a way I can't keep from noticing.

"Have you ever been to Florida?" I ask as we make our way down the steps to the tarmac below.

She shakes her head. "Like I said, I haven't traveled much. The farthest I've been from Seattle is California. I have family in the Bay Area."

She continues looking around in awe as we make our way to the car Marcus had arranged for us. Suddenly a feeling of satisfaction courses through me. A happiness that it turned out to be Ella in this whole arrangement. Despite the fact that she was so originally against it, I'm happy that she's the one who gets to go on this vacation. Just from the look on her face as she gazes out the car window, I know she's going to love this trip.

About forty-five minutes later, our car pulls up to a marina on the coast. Ella's eyes turn saucer-like as we approach the dock lined with yachts. And not just any yachts—enormous yachts. Yachts meant to sail the seas, yachts that can hold dozens of people.

Our chauffer leads us to the end of the dock where the largest yacht sits, and one by one, we board across the railed plank between the dock and the yacht.

"This is ... huge," Ella whispers as we make our way inside what looks to be one of three or four floors. Inside, Marcus and his wife are sitting on a pair of couches by a window overlooking a view of the ocean.

Marcus grins when he sees us, standing and opening his arms in greeting. "Welcome!" he calls, striding toward us. He shakes my and my brothers' hands, then looks to Olivia, Lilly, and Ella. "You three must be the better halves of these gentlemen."

Olivia laughs, holding out her hand. "I'm Olivia, Asher's wife."

Lilly introduces herself as well, and then Marcus turns to Ella. "And ... Ella, is it? I remember meeting you."

Ella holds out her hand in greeting. "Yes," she says with a warm smile. "So nice to see you again."

I'm impressed by her composure. She doesn't seem nervous at all—quite the feat considering all she's had to deal with today.

I notice who I assume is Julia striding up behind Marcus. "Please," Marcus says, turning to her. "Meet my wife, Julia."

"So nice to meet with you all. Marcus has told me wonderful things about you three," she says to my brothers and I. "And I'm excited to have some girl time with you ladies," she directs at the women.

We stand around engaging in small talk for a few minutes before Marcus instructs one of his employees to show us to our rooms. "Meet us out on the middle floor deck for some drinks whenever you're ready," he says in parting before we're shown down a staircase to the floor where our rooms are.

The steward takes us to our rooms where our luggage is waiting. Our rooms are all next to each other, and after saying a temporary goodbye to my family, Ella and I step inside ours.

She crosses the room and immediately heads to the balcony. She throws open the sliding glass door and steps out into the breeze, gazing out at the ocean. She spins around, a huge smile on her face.

"This is insane," she declares with a giggle, spinning back around to admire the view.

That flicker of happiness returns just by witnessing her joy. I watch her for a moment, caught up in her happiness. My mind wanders back to the plane ride, just a few short hours ago. How her soft body had felt pressed against mine, my arm wrapped around her shoulders. The smell of her hair. Strawberry? Fuck. The memory of it does something to me I'm unfamiliar with. Am I actually *attracted* to her? This barely-out-of-college girl who I haven't even acknowledged until now?

While she had been the one to sit up and pull away on the plane, it was probably for the best. I probably could have sat like that for hours—the entire plane ride. Just reveling in the feeling of her against me.

I shake my head, trying to rid myself of these thoughts, and turn to assess the luggage. "I'm going to change before we meet everyone on the deck for drinks," I say.

"Okay. I'm going to upback a bit," Ella says, returning to the room. She props her suitcase up on the bed and opens it. She rummages through a few things, finally pulling out the sandals I'd sent her. She turns it to me, a questioning look on her face. "These seem okay?" she asks.

I nod.

I pick out a new outfit, deciding to don a pair of khaki shorts and a nice short-sleeved button up instead of my dress slacks and long-sleeved shirt I'm currently wearing. Once I've emerged from the bathroom, I see Ella leaning down to clasp her sandals around her ankles. I subtly eyeing her up and down. Fuck she looks good in that dress. While it's definitely classy and modest, it does show off her arms and legs, parts of her I've never seen thanks to the gloomy Seattle weather.

Once I'm dressed, we leave our cabin and head up the stairs to the second floor. We cross the room we'd originally met Marcus and Julia in, and head out onto an uncovered deck filled with lounge chairs, a few tables, and a bar. Marcus and Julia are sitting in a cluster of chairs under an umbrella at the edge of the deck and call out in greeting when they see us.

"What are you drinks of choice?" Marcus asks warmly as we sit down.

"I'll have a gin and tonic," I say, turning to Ella questioningly.

"Uh … rum and coke?" she asks.

The waiter nods and heads off.

"Ella, that is a gorgeous dress," Julia says.

Ella smiles, a small blush creeping up her cheeks. I can tell she's slightly uncomfortable—maybe nervous. "Thanks," she says. "Alec bought it for me." She glances to me.

I smile at her, reaching out to gently place my hand on her arm. I mean it in a comforting way, but the touch only seems to electrify both her and I. I immediately drop my arm.

Thankfully, Aiden and Lilly make an appearance, sitting down beside us. A few minutes later, Olivia and Asher appear, and soon we're all engaged in conversation. Ella seems to relax now that the attention is spread evenly amongst us. I even notice her falling into a side conversation with Lilly and Olivia, seemingly hitting it off. I'm grateful that my sisters-in-law are being as welcoming as they are. Although I wouldn't expect otherwise—they're two of the nicest people I've ever met. It's truly a wonder how my brothers managed to score them.

I notice a staff member appear, and he comes up to Marcus's side. "We're ready to depart," he informs him.

"Good, yes. Let's get going. Thank you, Damien," Marcus replies.

"Off we go," Julia says to the rest of us with a broad smile. "We'll be in the Bahamas the day after tomorrow."

We all smile, and the chatter escalates, expressing our excitement for the trip. I stare off toward the shore as our boat slowly pushes away from the dock and begins making its way out into open waters. I take a deep breath, glancing surreptitiously at Ella. Here we go, indeed. Hopefully we can pull this off.

Chapter 9

Ella

The warmth of the sun caresses my skin, a soft ocean breeze whisking through my hair. Olivia, Lilly, and I are all seated around the small pool on the top deck of the yacht as the boat sails through the open waters. Leaning back on the lounge chair, I stare out at the ocean. I've never seen waters like this. I've never seen anything like this. I never thought I'd be sailing on a multi-million-dollar yacht to the Bahamas. In a swimsuit that probably cost more than my rent. Somebody pinch me.

And so far, our ruse seems to be working. We'd spent the rest of yesterday casually chatting over dinner and drinks. And unlike the horror stories I'd imagined—Marcus drilling us on the details of our relationship—conversation seemed to flow naturally. Which is obvious, now that I think about it. I'm sure that my relationship with Alec is the least of either Marcus or Juila's concerns. In fact, I've spent most of my time talking with Olivia and Lilly, who obviously know about our fake relationship, so it takes quite a bit of the pressure off.

"I swear, Asher was so excited to spend a week away from work, and now what does he do?" Olivia says with a laugh. "Talk about work."

Lilly rolls her eyes. "It's all three of them. And Marcus Caddelle too, by the looks of him."

"Something in their blood," Olivia bemoans.

It's then that Lilly turns to me, eyeing me tentatively for a moment before venturing, "So, how are things going with you and Alec?"

I raise my eyebrows, somewhat surprised by the question. "Um. Fine. I mean, I think we're pulling it off okay." Then, suddenly beginning to doubt myself, I add, "Do you?"

Olivia snorts. "Oh yeah. You guys are definitely playing the part convincingly."

"Oh. Good," I answer, relieved.

"When I first heard about all this, I was worried, to be honest." Lilly admits. "Alec isn't exactly known for his … warmth. I mean, he's nice to the people he cares about, but he's not a great actor."

I nod. "Yeah, tell me about it."

At this, Olivia raises an eyebrow.

I chuckle, feeling that I can open up to these women, at least somewhat. I mean, what's the worst that could happen? It gets back to Alec? So what? After this week, I'll never see any of these people ever again. Other than Alec when I stop by to walk Betty. And he's barely there anyway. "I always thought he was a bit of an asshole," I admit. "In fact, he insulted me *right* before accidentally introducing me as his wife and then begging me to play the part."

Olivia bursts into laughter. "God. Alec."

"Sounds like something he'd do," Lilly agrees.

"Tell us if he's ever too much. We'll put him in his place," Olivia promises.

I laugh, but I'm also actually grateful for the sentiment. Knowing that I have someone willing to be on my side this week, out at sea in the middle of nowhere—it means a lot. And after having learned more about Olivia and Lilly the past few hours, it's nice to be surrounded by people more … like me. At first, I'd assumed the other Mrs. Kings came from money just like the guys. But Olivia and Lilly are normal people. With normal jobs, and normal lives. Well, until meeting their husbands. But they have a grounded air about them that I find comforting.

And it's good to hear that Alec and I are seemingly pulling it off. And if our vacation continues like this—the boys off discussing business, and the girls hanging out by the pool—it'll be easier than I thought.

Chapter 10

Alec

"Enough shop talk," Marcus insists as we make our way along the outer deck of the yacht. "Maybe finding those wives of yours will help shut this down."

Asher and Aiden laugh along good naturedly. But as much as we're all ready to enjoy some cool drinks by the pool, the five of us—Marcus, Julia, Asher, Aiden, and I—had had quite the productive conversation about the future of our companies. The merger seems to be happening—for real. I could pinch myself. And I know Asher and Aiden are feeling the same way.

We round the corner and make our way up a staircase to the top deck where the pool is. I hear

Olivia and Lilly call out in greeting as the others reach the top of the stairs first. As I climb up behind them, the top deck coming into view, my eyes immediately land on Ella.

And my jaw about falls to the floor. She's wearing one of the swimsuits I'd gotten her. It's a white one-piece. Unsure of her comfortability and not wanting to seem creepy, I hadn't sent her any bikinis. Although I hadn't been wholly aware of how *sexy* a one-piece could be. At least on her.

The cut of the suit is high around her hips, accentuating her slim waist and curves. Her skin glistens in the sun, her auburn hair falling in loose waves over her shoulders.

Fuck, she looks good.

"Now that's the way a newlywed looks at his wife." Marcus chuckles, slapping me on the back.

Stunned back to reality, I quickly turn my gaze away from Ella, laughing along with Marcus, nodding and trying to hide the blush I'm worried is creeping up my cheeks. I'm not sure if Ella overheard the comment, but I'm suddenly self-conscious and hyperaware of my every move.

Aiden has already sidled up to Lilly, sharing her lounger chair with her and pulling her into his lap. Asher plants a kiss on Olivia's cheek as he pulls up a chair beside her. Damn. I hadn't thought about how my brothers' affections toward their wives would affect how I look interacting with Ella.

Trying not to look stiff as a board, I take a seat in the empty chair beside Ella, reaching over to gently give her arm a squeeze in greeting. She smiles shyly back.

"So, what have you ladies been up to?" Julia asks.

"Just lounging around, getting some sun," Lilly answers.

The conversation shifts to hobbies and pastimes, then to Olivia and Asher's anniversary plans a few months out. "We'd been thinking of the Bahamas, but it seems like we're already knocking that one out," Asher says with a laugh.

Julia suggests Aruba, to which Olivia inquires more about. After a few minutes of chatter, Marcus veers the conversation back to me. "Alec, you said you and Ella are the most recently married couple—when did you get married?"

"July," I answer, shooting Ella a smile the way a newlywed would.

"July what?"

"The 20th," I say off the top of my head.

"How sweet," Julia chimes in. "So you're about six months in."

"In fact," Marcus says, glancing down at his phone. "It's exactly six months! It's January 20th today." He laughs in surprise, as do the rest of us— although somewhat halfheartedly. "Lauren!" he calls to a server near the end of the deck. "Bring us all some champagne, please." He turns back to us. "This calls for a toast."

I laugh, trying to wave it off. "No, please."

"Oh, why not?" Marcus presses. "We're in the Caribbean, on vacation, and you two just happen to be exactly six months into your marriage. Why not celebrate?"

I suppose he's got a point. Why not? Although I'm not exactly loving the extra attention. And I can tell Ella isn't either. But she's got a grin painted on her face anyway.

A few moments later, Lauren comes with a tray of champagne flutes, passing them out to each of us. "To Alec and Ella," Marcus declares, raising his glass. We all follow suit. "To a long and happy marriage."

We clink glasses and all take a sip. Ella giggles somewhat nervously under all the attention before taking her sip.

"You two are the sweetest," Julia comments from beside us. "Kiss, why don't you?"

Ella's eyes go just a tad bit wider at this, and a bolt of electricity shoots through me—from anticipation or dread, though, I'm unsure.

"Oh, we don't have to—" I start.

"Oh, yes!" Marcus chimes in. He holds his flute up high again. "Kiss!" He gestures with his hands.

Feeling my face redden, I turn to Ella. She looks just as uncomfortable as I feel, but when I raise my eyebrow in a silent question, she shrugs a shoulder, seemingly understanding just as well as I do that Marcus and Julia won't take no for an answer. Simply kissing is going to be our fastest way out of this.

"Kiss, kiss, kiss," Marcus chants jovially, and Julia chimes in. Then I hear a third voice and glance over in annoyance to see that Aiden has joined in. He only laughs harder when he notices my irritation. Asshole.

I turn back to Ella, chuckling at the absurdity of this. I reach for her, gently cupping my hand at the back of her neck. Her hair is soft between my fingers—

softer than I thought it would be. Nerves dance in her eyes, and I wish I hadn't put her in this situation, but here we are. Closing my eyes, I slowly lean toward her. My lips brush against hers, tentatively at first, as though I might crush her if I were to kiss her too hard. Her lips are impossibly soft, a sensation I'm unsure if I've ever felt before. Sure, I've obviously kissed before, but it's never quite felt like *this*.

She kisses me back slowly, her lips moving against mine in a hypnotic page. I feel my cock pulse in my pants, and I'm suddenly overcome with an urge to wrap her up in my arms, to devour her, to make her mine right here and now, but before I can act on it, I abruptly pull back.

Ella opens her eyes, staring up at me with wide eyes.

"Now that's the kiss of a newly wedded couple," Julia says with a chuckle.

Ella pulls away from me, giggling slightly and brushing her hair behind her ear. Snapping out of it, I simply grin good naturedly at everyone, quickly bringing my champagne flute to my mouth and drinking. I down it in just a few seconds, hoping nobody notices.

The conversation quickly picks back up, with Asher and Olivia discussing alternative anniversary trip destinations. I glance sideways at Ella, but she refuses to meet my gaze. Out of embarrassment or irritation, I'm not sure. We did agree that kissing was only on the table in an absolutely necessary moment. But I can't quite think of a moment more necessary than that.

Either way, I have a slightly more pressing issue at hand. Something that's been creeping into the back of my mind—much faster than expected—and making a nice, little home. Ella, the dogwalker I never paid a second glance to, has somehow turned into something absolutely irresistible. And now that I've kissed her ...

I'm fucked.

Chapter 11

Ella

The light to our cabin flicks on as I push open the door and step inside, Alec just a few paces behind me. The view out our balcony is pitch black as the sun set a few hours ago. The lamps on the walls cast a warm light throughout the room.

Alec sits down on the couch with a sigh, reaching down to unlace his shoes. I sit on the bed, suddenly aware of a hint of awkwardness in the air. I glance sideways at Alec, but he isn't looking at me. I can't tell if he's avoiding eye contact on purpose, or if his shoes are just being particularly difficult to untie right now.

We haven't been alone together all day. Not since this morning, and not since we kissed in the presence of everyone on board just a few hours ago.

My face warms just thinking about it. I kissed Alec King. And not only kissed him, but *kissed* him. I'd panicked internally when I'd seen where the conversation was going, knowing that we'd be peer pressured into kissing. I'd been fine with it, assuming it would be a simple peck. But the sensation of his lips against mine had somehow driven every other thought from my brain, and all I'd wanted was for that kiss to continue—for how long, I can't say. And apparently Alec had felt the same, because I remember the way his fingers had wrapped themselves up in my hair against the back of my neck, how he'd deepened the kiss, how he'd ever so slightly pulled me toward him.

"Ella," Alec's voice pulls me from my thoughts with a start.

I turn toward him.

"Sorry about … earlier," he says with a shake of his head. "I just wanted to check in. Are you okay?"

I raise my eyebrows. "Oh. Yeah. Of course."

"I know we agreed that kissing was kind of a last resort, but I just didn't know how to get out of … that." Alec chuckles, and I do too, thinking of the boisterous Marcus and Julia. Their actions would be sweet if we truly were a married couple.

"Yeah, there really was no way around it," I agree. "And it's fine. Really."

He nods, pinning me to the spot with that gaze of his. "Good. I just wanted to make sure things were … good. I guess."

"Things are good," I assure him.

An uncomfortable silence passes between us. I kick off my sandals and pull my feet up onto the bed, shifting a bit. I glance toward the window, but there's nothing to see but blackness, so I look back at my lap.

"Are you having a good time?" Alec asks, seemingly just to break the awkward silence that's permeating the room.

I look up. "Yeah. I've never been anywhere like this before," I say with a genuine smile.

A ghost of a smile plays on his lips. "You seem to be hitting it off with Olivia and Lilly."

I nod. "Yeah, they're sweet. I like them a lot."

"That's good," he replies. "I'm glad they're being welcoming. I know you're doing this all for me because of our agreement—and as a *huge* favor—but I truly do want you to enjoy yourself." I'm surprised at the genuineness of his statement. He's actually being … nice. Sure, I never thought Alec King was the devil or anything, but he's also never been the kindest person around. And this whole arrangement? It was just to get him the biggest deal of his career and get him out of a stupid mistake he'd made. That was all. To hear that he actually cares about my feelings this week? It might be small, but it feels like a big win in Alec King territory.

"Are *you* enjoying yourself?" I ask.

He seems surprised by the question, and maybe even more surprised as to how to answer. "I—I mean, I guess," he answers.

I laugh. "You guess? You're on a yacht headed to the Bahamas."

A soft grin washes over his face, and he nods absentmindedly. "True."

"I mean, the merger is pretty much solidified, right?" I press.

He shrugs. "Seems to be that way, but you never know."

"And is relaxing and having a good time going to stop any potential disasters from throwing the merger off course?" I tease.

At this, he shoots me a look—a cross between annoyance and acceptance. "No, I suppose not."

"In fact, knowing Marcus, I think letting loose might just *increase* your chances of a successful merger happening."

At this, he chuckles. "Yeah, Marcus does seem to value 'letting loose,' as you say."

"So I ask again: Are you enjoying yourself?"

He meets my gaze, a long pause passing between us, and suddenly I'm thrown back to just a few hours ago and how it had felt to have his lips pressed against mine, our bodies closer than they've ever been. Is he thinking about that too? Is he just as affected by that kiss as I was? Or am I just a hopeless little schoolgirl, barely of out college, getting caught up in the glitz and glamor of Alec King and his empire?

"Yes, Ella," he says evenly. "I'd say I'm enjoying myself." His words are slow, his dark eyes somehow darker, and I feel my insides melting.

My heart beats just a little faster, and somehow I'm having a hard time catching my breath. But before I asphyxiate on the spot, Alec clears his throat, breaking our eye contact and standing. "I'm going to get ready for bed," he says, grabbing his pajamas off the couch and heading into the bathroom.

As soon as I hear the door click, I lay back on the mattress, letting out a long exhale. *Keep it together, Ella*, I tell myself, closing my eyes. Alec King might be my husband for the week, but he is a hundred percent off limits.

Chapter 12

Ella

The boat docks at the Bahamas the next day in the early afternoon. I stand on the deck watching as we near the island, the palm trees and perfect white sand visible from far away. I watch in awe, taking it all in. After docking, Marcus and Julia suggest that we go ashore and enjoy some time on a private beach nearby. So, after changing and gathering our things for the day, we all disembark, taking a taxi to a beach with cabanas and a gorgeous stretch of sand and pristine water.

I immediately make a beeline to the ocean, wading through the waves and sinking in. I float, closing my eyes and soaking up the sun and waves. Lilly joins me for a while, and we bob with the waves while the others lay about on covered loungers.

"So, that *kiss* yesterday ..." Lilly says with a wiggle of her eyebrows.

I feel a blush creeping up my cheeks. "Yeah, that was ..." I laugh.

"Sorry about Aiden joining in on the egging on, by the way. I definitely chewed him out later for that." She shakes her head.

"Oh, it's fine. It's what I signed up for. We are 'married' after all," I tell her.

"You're being a good sport about this whole thing."

I shrug. "Yeah, what can I say? I have a high tolerance for cruising through Caribbean waters and chilling in the Bahamas."

Lilly chuckles.

We spend the rest of the day on the beach, and while I filter in and out of the water, joining the others from time to time, I can't help but notice something just a bit off about Alec. Is it just me, or is he avoiding me? Unlike his brothers, he doesn't save a seat for me under the cabana, and he doesn't make room for me when I approach. He's also been avoiding the water like the plague. Is it because that's where I'm spending most of my time, or is he just some sort of germaphobe or something?

Either way, I decide not to let it bother me on what might possibly be the best day of my life. I've never seen water this color of turquoise before. I spend hours striding along the shoreline searching for shells, stooping to inspect small sea creatures, and tossing pebbles into the water.

As the sun begins to slowly descend upon the horizon, I turn to see Olivia jogging up the beach toward me. I hadn't realized how far I'd wandered from the group.

"Hey," she says when she gets within earshot. "We're all heading back to the boat now. We're going to change and grab dinner at a nice restaurant Marcus knows."

"Sounds good," I say, and we fall into step side by side as we head back to the others. After a few steps, I summon the courage to ask, "Is Alec okay? He seems off today."

"More off than he's been the whole trip?" Olivia asks with a chuckle.

I offer her a questioning look.

She smirks. "He's definitely off. Whether it's nerves about being able to pull off this charade or nerves about something else, I don't know."

Something else? What else? Probably the whole merger with Marcus's company, I decide. And maybe I'm just imagining things about today in particular. It's not like we know each other that well. Or at all. Who am I to say Alec is acting weird?

We take a car back to the yacht and make our way to our rooms. Once inside, Alec silently opens his suitcase, pulling out what appears to be dress slacks and a button down. "Wear one of the nicer dresses I sent you," he says over his shoulder. "It sounds like this place is one of the nicest on the island."

I nod, rummaging through my bag until I find one. I choose a deep red dress that falls just below my knees. I head to the bathroom. I take a quick shower, quickly blow drying my hair just enough so that it will dry with some loose curls, and put on a bit of makeup—mascara and some lip gloss.

Then I grab the red dress. I slip it on, the satin silky and soft against my skin. I turn from side to side to view myself in the mirror. It's a cute dress—a gorgeous dress, actually. I have to admit that Alec has good taste. I reach behind me to pull up the zipper. I make it halfway up my back before realizing there's also a corset-style tie that needs to be woven along my mid back. I turn around, craning my neck over my shoulder to try to see my reflection in the mirror, struggling with the ties.

After a few moments, I sigh in frustration. There's no way I'm going to be able to tie this up myself. Which only means one thing.

I suck in a deep breath and exit the bathroom hesitantly.

Alec is standing in the room already dressed, fiddling with a watch on his wrist. I look him up and down. He looks showered.

He turns to me. Noticing my quizzical gaze, he says, "I used the shower in an empty cabin next to us." Then he takes in my dress, his eyes slowly devouring the length of me. I try not to let myself blush.

"I, uh ... actually, could you help me fasten the back?" I ask timidly.

Is it just me, or do Alec's eyes widen slightly? Either way, his expression is immediately back to neutral, and he simply nods.

I spin around, holding the front of my dress to my chest and waiting patiently for him to tie me up. He steps up behind me, and I can feel his breath on the back of my neck. I shudder instinctively.

He reaches for the ties of my dress, his fingers gently brushing against the bare skin of my back. He clears his throat. "This is a ridiculous design for a dress," he comments.

"You're the one who bought it."

He doesn't respond, simply begins weaving the ties through the fabric on either side of the open back and cinching it with a bow. "There," he says, gently patting my back, his touch lingering just a tad longer than needed.

I turn back around. "Thank you," I say quietly.

He nods, avoiding eye contact. "Ready to go?"

"Sure." I dig out a pair of wedge sandals from my bag, grab my purse from the countertop, and follow Alec out the door.

"Oooh, don't you look pretty," Lilly says, coming out of her room across the hall.

"Thank you," I say, sidling up to her. I wish those words had come from Alec, but I'll take them from Lilly too.

Asher and Olivia exit their room as well, and all of us make our way to the middle deck where the ramp to the dock is. I find myself walking with Lilly as we all make our way to a car waiting for us at the base of the pier. I even sit next to her in the car, with Alec sitting up front near Marcus.

Whatever. It's not like it really matters whether he pays me attention or not. And the stakes of this charade fall fully to him. I'm being paid to be here no matter what, I rationalize. Determined to not let whatever weird tension is in the air get to me, I stare out the window at the setting sun as we make our way to the restaurant.

Once we arrive, I understand why Alec requested I wear my nicest dress. This place is *fancy*. The servers are dressed to the nines, and the seating area juts out over the water, offering a gorgeous view of the ocean bathed in the sunset.

The host leads us to a table on the deck. I make myself sit next to Alec, knowing it would be weird if I were to sit somewhere else. Even though I'd rather spend the evening chatting with Lilly. We order drinks and fall into casual conversation. Alec begins speaking with Marcus and Julia to his right, turning his back to me just enough that I feel as though entering the conversation myself would be an intrusion.

I glance left at Asher and Olivia, but they seem to be caught up in a conversation with Aiden and Lilly about something I have nothing to add to. So I sit in silence, glancing around the restaurant. When the server sets our drinks down, I gratefully take mine and bring it to my lips, taking a sip. This already feels like it's going to be a long night.

Marcus and Julia insist that this restaurant is known for their fish, so I order some kind of salmon dish, as does most everyone else. When the food arrives, I pick at it slowly. It's amazing, just as they'd promised, but I can't help but feel the tension leaking off of Alec to my right. Is something *wrong*?

Part of me wonders if others can feel this too. Maybe Marcus and Julia think we're fighting. Or worse—they know this is all a complete sham. Should I try to initiate some sort of conversation?

But what the hell am I thinking? Alec is the one who wanted this. Who proposed this and went ahead with this scheme. It's up to him to do the legwork here.

Frustrated, I take a big bite of salmon and chew.

"So, Olivia," Julia says, diverting her attention across the table. "Asher tells us you play a vital role in the company."

Olivia smiles humbly. "I oversee administration," she says. She talks for a bit about how she started at the company and her dedication to its mission. She never really saw herself in tech, but has been loving it nonetheless.

"And Lilly, you run one of King Tech's nonprofits?" Julia asks after Olivia has finished.

"I do." Lilly beams. "The Maria King Foundation. It offers art programs for kids in the Seattle community, as well as hosting art shows displaying local talent."

"So fascinating," Julia says, and the two of them talk about art and philanthropic endeavors for a while.

Apparently, Julia has goals of starting a nonprofit herself.

"And what about you, Ella? I don't think Alec has told us what you do," Julia finally turns to me.

Startled, I put my glass down. "Oh. I, uh ..."

But Alec beats me to it. Placing a hand over my own and squeezing gently, he says, "Oh, Ella is the perfect, little housewife."

I look at him, somewhat surprised. I guess we hadn't really discussed this part, but I kind of just assumed that if asked, I'd tell the truth. I just graduated college, and I'm planning on going to vet school.

But maybe that isn't fitting for a wife of Alec's stature.

"A noble calling," Julia says, and I can tell she means it. And it's not that I disagree, it's just not ... me. And what would being a housewife to Alec King entail? Surely nothing like being a normal housewife. I'm sure he has people to do everything for him. So where would that leave me? Lounging around and doing nothing? It's not like we even have kids in this story.

"I love nothing more than to simply take care of her," Alec goes on, clasping my hand in his and bringing it to his lips for a quick kiss.

He force myself to smile.

The conversation quickly flits to something else. Unlike Olivia and Lilly, there isn't much to discuss about me. Only, there is. I have goals, dreams, plans I'm excited about it. And I know this is all just a charade and I'll never see these people again, but I don't know if I've ever felt smaller than in this single moment. Sitting next to the richest and most accomplished people I've ever met, and being presented as a young, naïve girl who simply lives off her older husband's hard work.

I know this isn't real. But it still feels like shit anyway.

The dinner ends with another round of wine, and I down mine a bit faster than normal. By the time we're all heading back to the yacht, I'm a tad bit wobbly on my heels. Although that might be from the fact that I never wear heels.

It's late by the time we get back to the boat, so most of us head to bed. I'm exhausted anyway.

I immediately flip my heels off when I enter the room, sighing deeply and tossing my purse on the counter.

Alec sits down to untie his shoes in silence. The tension in the air is getting to me, but I try my hardest not to let it show.

"Did you have a nice dinner?" Alec asks without looking up.

I roll my eyes, but I know he doesn't notice. "It was nice," I say flatly.

He looks up. "Did you not like it?"

"I said I liked it."

He frowns. "You're not acting like you just had a nice dinner. You're acting like …"

"Like you've been ignoring me all day?" I finish for him.

Realization washes over his face, and he slowly nods. "Oh. Okay. So that's why you're upset."

"I'm not upset," I shoot back, although I realize the futility in that action. Which only angers me more.

"You're upset," he insists, and it's like I can feel the rage literally building up inside of me.

"I'm weirded out by the fact that you've been avoiding me all day. And then you sit there at dinner and basically paint me like some helpless little girl who you just take care of—like I don't have a life of my own. I know none of this is real, but is that really what you'd want in a wife?"

Alec locks taken aback. His eyebrows furrow, and his mouth drops open slightly.

"Your brothers' wives are accomplished, interesting people. And *yours* apparently just sits around at home all day being the 'perfect, little housewife,' like some type of pet."

"I didn't mean it like that," Alec interjects, his voice hard.

"Well then why didn't you let me answer, then? Because I could have told them I'm more than just arm candy."

"I'm sure they don't think that."

"I don't know what they think. I don't know what anyone thinks. Olivia and Lilly have been nice to me, but I don't know them. They probably think this entire situation is insane—which it is—and are just politely passing the time with me. I'm in the middle of the ocean, alone, with a bunch of strangers, and the only person I know *even a little bit* here has spent the whole day avoiding me." My rant comes to an abrupt end, and I take in a deep breath of air, sighing angrily.

Holy shit, I'm actually upset. I'm actually *hurt* by this. I can feel a lump in my throat, but I shove it down. I blink, looking away.

Alec stands, taking a step toward me. "You think I didn't let you speak at dinner because I think less of you?"

I force myself to meet his gaze, to stare defiantly back at him.

"I didn't let you speak because you're not obligated to share personal information about yourself to strangers I strongarmed you into meeting," he answers. "And I've been giving you space today because I thought that's what you would want after yesterday."

"Because kissing me was so horrible," I snap before I can stop myself.

His expression hardens, and he takes another step closer, his body now barely a foot from mine, towering over me. I refuse to step back, instead, staring right back at him.

"That kiss yesterday—was that the kiss of a man who wasn't enjoying himself?" he asks slowly, pinning me to the spot with his gaze.

I swallow, remembering the way he'd pressed his lips against mine as if he'd wanted more but had refrained. "I don't know," I finally whisper.

"Yes you do, Ella," he murmurs. "You know it, and I know it. You know that kiss yesterday wasn't *just* for show. You know I was avoiding you today because all I wanted was to do it again. And you know that it's taking everything inside of me right now not to push you back onto this bed and absolutely devour you."

Adrenaline spikes through me, and I can feel a hot flush creeping across my skin. Alec's eyes bore into mine, and I couldn't look away even if I wanted to. My heart is racing out of control, but the only thing I can think about is the idea of pressing my body against his and giving into every urge flitting through my head.

"What's stopping you?" The words come out hushed, shaky, as if I could break this delicate moment in half. "I'm your wife, after all."

Alec's gaze drops to my lips, then back up. And then, as if flipping a switch, he reaches out to grasp my face between his hands, pulling my lips to his. Unlike our kiss yesterday, this one is hard, desperate, as if his very life depends on it. And as if mine does too, I kiss him back.

We stumble backward, toward the bed, the backs of my knees hitting the mattress. Without breaking our kiss, Alec pushes me backward, crawling up over me as I lay back on the bed, his hands tangling in my hair. I reach down to hike my dress high enough so I can wrap my legs around him as he settles between them. His body presses down on mine, the weight of him sending a frenzy of fire through my lower belly.

He breaks our kiss to trail kisses down the side of my face, my neck, softly nibbling. I sigh as his hands leave my hair and travel down my body, over the satin of my dress, over my breasts and stomach. I can feel my nipples hardening under his touch, and with no bra, I know he can feel it as well.

His mouth is back on mine, kissing me deeply, his tongue passing my lips and tangling with mine. He gently squeezes my breasts, then runs his thumbs over my nipples, and I moan softly into his mouth, arching my back, desperate for more.

Suddenly, though, he breaks the kiss, sitting up slightly, a look of uncertainty washing across his face. "Ella," he breathes, searching my eyes. "Should we— are you okay with—"

I reach up to grasp the collar of his shirt, pulling him back down. "Shut up and fuck me," I order. I don't know where the words came from or how I had the audacity to let them spill from my mouth, but they're the most honest words I've uttered this entire trip. I need Alec. I need him now.

He doesn't need more convincing than that. He lowers his lips to my throat, kissing and sucking his way down my neck, my collarbone, and to the tops of my breasts. Sitting up just slightly, he gently slides the spaghetti straps of my dress over my shoulders, tugging the top of my dress down slowly until my breasts are exposed.

He stares down at me for a moment, taking a shuddering breath as he runs his hands over them, gently teasing my nipples. I close my eyes, leaning my head back against the mattress and arching my back, pressing my breasts against his palms. I feel him lower his mouth, taking one of my nipples and sucking, flicking his tongue over it again and again.

I moan, tangling my fingers in his hair. He spends his time here, caressing my nipples with his hands and mouth until they're red and swollen and I'm a whimpering puddle on the bed.

I reach for his shirt, hastily undoing the top buttons. He helps, and within a few seconds, his button-up lies discarded on the floor. His chest is sculpted, and I run my hands over it, down across his abs. He stands, swiftly unzipping his dress pants and stepping out of them, holding my eye contact the whole time. I sit up on my elbows, my thin red dress bunched around my waist. When he lowers his boxers, that's when I break our gaze, glancing downward. My mouth parts, and my eyes widen.

Alec is definitely ... big. Not unmanageable, but definitely bigger than I've ever taken. Completely naked, Alec stalks toward the bed and climbs back over me. He presses me back down against the mattress, his hand snaking between my legs, under my panties, to find my center. I gasp as he runs a finger over my clit, creating slow, gentle circles.

He leans back just far enough to hook his fingers under the waistband of my panties on either side of my hips and slowly slide them off my legs. And then there I am, completely bare, my legs spread before him. He stares down at my center long enough to make me blush.

And then he settles between my legs, pressing his body against mine, his gaze hardened with desire as it meets mine. I wrap my legs around him, and I can feel him positioning himself at my entrance.

I take in a shuddering breath, and then slowly, he enters me.

I gasp at the sensation of being stretched, of feeling fuller than I ever have before. As he sinks deeper into me, he presses his mouth to my ear. "Good girl," he murmurs, and I hear myself whimper, becoming even wetter and allowing him fully into me. Taking all of me at once—every inch.

He slowly begins thrusting in and out of me, and I cling to him desperately.

"You're so beautiful," he whispers, kissing my neck, right behind my ear. He runs his hands over my body, my sides, my breasts, as he continues thrusting. "So perfect."

I moan as he picks up speed, pinning me to the bed with his weight. He thrusts harder, and I cry out in pleasure. Alec quickly covers my mouth with his palm. "Shhhh," he murmurs. "Be a good girl and be quiet."

Fuck. Him calling me *good girl* is turning my insides to jelly. All I want is to hear him say it over and over again. "Be your good, little wife, huh?" I reply breathlessly when he removes his hand from my mouth.

The corner of his mouth quirks up in a smirk. "How about you be an obedient wife and come for me?" He snakes a hand between us, reaching lower until he finds my aching bud.

As soon as he does, a deep moan escapes me, and I buck my hips.

"That's it," he praises, pumping harder.

I grip the bedsheets beside me, whimpering desperately as he picks up speed—both in thrusting and in fingering my clit. "Oh, god," I pant.

"Come for me, Ella," Alec demands. "Be a good girl and do what I say."

I never thought I'd enjoy being bossed around in bed, but his words are having an effect on me that I've never experienced before. The pleasure inside me is building and building, and with a strangled cry, my orgasm shudders through me.

Almost instantly, Alec finishes as well, collapsing on top of me. We lay there in silence, panting. The waves of my orgasm begin to diminish, and as the fog clears from my brain, I suddenly realize what I've just done. What we've just done.

Alec is lying on top of me, still inside of me, his naked body pressed against mine. And we just fucked. And I don't know whether to laugh or cry. All I know is that this trip just became a whole lot more complicated.

Chapter 13

Alec

Sunlight streams through the curtains, nudging me awake. I stretch, and it takes me a few moments to register where I am. Not in my penthouse apartment in Seattle, but on a yacht docked in the Bahamas. And not on the couch where I've slept the past few nights, but in the bed. Next to Ella.

Ella.

I turn my head to see her sleeping form curled up against me, her arm thrown over my bare chest. Holy shit. Ella. Tucked against me, her bare back exposed to the room, her body gently rises and falls as she breathes, deep asleep. Her brown, wavy hair is strewn across the pillow, and I resist the urge to reach out and caress it, worried any movement will wake her up.

This morning, in the light of day, a mild panic takes hold of me. Because everything has changed. Well, I guess not technically in regards to the charade we're trying to pull off. But everything in regards to me and Ella's actual relationship. What the hell was I thinking? Jeopardizing everything in the name of lust? Although if I'm honest with myself, it might have been more than simple lust. Because there's something about Ella. Something that drives me crazy but warms my heart at the same time. And last night, she'd been too irresistible to deny.

And so here we are.

She shifts against me, and I freeze. But despite my attempt not to wake her, she stretches lazily, blinking her eyes open. Just like me, it seems to take her a moment to gauge her surroundings, and when she angles her head up toward mine, there's a bit of hesitance in her eyes.

"Morning," I greet her.

"Good morning," she replies with the ghost of a smile. She turns, peeling herself away from me. Realizing she's naked, she quickly covers her breasts, much to my disappointment. The breasts I'd spent last night becoming very, very acquainted with.

She wraps the sheet tightly around herself and stands. "I'm going to get ready for breakfast," she says, shooting me a look I can only describe as shy.

A far cry from the woman who told me to shut up and fuck her last night. Although the blush adorning her cheeks is utterly adorable. She pads into the bathroom with a pile of clothes.

I take the opportunity to clothe myself, grabbing a short-sleeved button up and a pair of shorts. I run my fingers through my hair and double check my appearance in the mirror.

Ella emerges a few minutes later, dressed, her hair combed, and the subtle scent of perfume in the air.

I smile at her. "Ready for breakfast?" I ask.

She nods. "Ready."

Everyone except for Olivia is already at breakfast when we arrive. The chef comes out to take our orders and then heads back to make it.

"Where's Olivia?" I ask Asher.

"She's not feeling super great," Asher responds. "I think just the rocking of the boat last night made her feel a little ill."

Julia nods along understandingly. "Yeah, even docked, the waves can really get to you if you're not used to them."

The conversation at the table turns to our plans for the day, and we all agree that spending another day lounging around at the beach would be worthwhile. After finishing breakfast, Asher goes to check on Olivia, and since she's feeling better, we all head out for a second day on the beach.

We head to another more secluded beach on the opposite side of the island today, outfitted with lounge chairs, umbrellas, along with snacks and beverages. The water here is just as blue and clear as the beach yesterday, if not more so. I watch as Ella busies herself strolling along the sand, watching as the waves crash, and then wading out to her chest, lying on her back and floating, staring up at the sky. I let her be for a while before the urge to join her overcomes me, and I find myself wading out into the water to meet her.

She must feel my presence, because she lifts her head and stands once I'm about five feet away.

"Hey," she greets with a shy smile.

"Hi," I say back, running my hands through the crystal clear water. I've noticed a tension between us today. Well, maybe not tension exactly. More like uncertainty. Hesitancy.

Waking up next to a naked Ella had been nothing short of amazing. And last night was …

I can't even think about it without turning myself on. But I don't know what Ella thinks. Now. Today, after time to clear her head and think about what we did. Hell, I barely know how I feel about it.

Other than the fact that I'd love to feel her soft body underneath mine again. In fact, I'm craving it.

"How are you doing today?" I ask.

She seems surprised by the question. "Good," she answers. "Loving this." She gestures to the view around us.

"How are you feeling about … last night?" I summon the courage to ask. A jolt of adrenaline spikes through me just at the thought of it.

She pauses, looking at me hesitantly. "How are *you* feeling about it?"

I chuckle softly. "I asked you first."

She smiles, looking down at the water. "I feel … good about it." She looks to meet my gaze, her eyes a mixture of trepidation and hope.

"Yeah?" I ask, stepping toward her.

Her smiles widens, although she's still acting shy. "Yeah," she says with a small shrug. "It was … *good*."

I reach for her under the water, grabbing her waist and tugging her toward me. "You're right, it was good," I agree.

Her cheeks go red.

"So you're not regretting anything?" I ask, surprising myself at how much I care about her response. I'm practically holding my breath, praying she'll say no.

She shakes her head. "No, not regretting anything. Are you?" A flicker of uncertainty shows on her face.

I tug her closer to me so that her chest is flush with mine, staring down at her. "Regretting?" I repeat. "If anything, I've spent the entirety of the day thinking about doing it again." I reach down to lightly lift her up, causing her to wrap her legs around my waist, floating in the water. I settle my arms around her waist, my hands at the small of her back. I nuzzle my face close to her ear. "And everything else I could do to you," I murmur.

"Yeah?" she breathes into my ear.

"Yeah," I reply. "Would you like that?" I nibble lightly on her ear. I glance over her shoulder, at the beach, at the lawn chairs about a hundred feet away where everyone else is sitting. They can barely see us from here, and even if they were looking, we just look like a normal husband and wife enjoying the ocean. There are a handful of others littered across the beach, but none of them are nearby.

Ella takes in a shuddering breath. I lean back to meet her gaze, and I grin at what I see there. Desperation, desire, need. She wants this as much as I do. And that's all I needed to know.

I position one of my hands under her ass, squeezing, holding her against me. My free hand snakes between us, pressing against her bare stomach and traveling slowly upward. I gently reach under her bikini top, cupping her bare breast beneath the water.

I slowly roll her nipple between my thumb and forefinger, causing her to suck in a breath of air. She ever so slightly arches her back, pressing her breasts toward me. I grin, positioning my hand to run my thumb over her nipple, over and over again.

She closes her eyes and sighs, leaning her head back slightly. I remove my hand and then tug the bikini top down so that it's bunched below her now-exposed breasts. I switch to her other breast, massaging her nipple and then pinching it lightly. I spend a few minutes alternating back and forth until Ella is practically panting, arching her back and whimpering.

I want her good and ready for me.

I move my hand from her breast and down, across her stomach, and then under her bikini bottoms. My finger slides along her slit, and even in the water, I can tell how wet she is. Fuck. I'm already hard just feeling it.

I slowly insert a finger inside of her, and her mouth opens in a perfect O. "Alec," she pants, glancing over her shoulder toward the shore. "We're in public."

I grin, responding by inserting a second finger inside of her and eliciting a soft cry from her. "What? You don't want any beachgoers to know that I'm pleasuring you? That you're panting and whimpering like a little slut?" The second comment is a bit of a risk, and I know it, but there's a spark that flashes in Ella's eyes right after I say it that tells me she's just as turned on by the dirty talk as I am. It makes my grin wider. Fuck, I'm going to have fun with her.

She bites her lip, suppressing a moan as I begin pumping my fingers in and out of her.

"No one's close enough to know what we're doing," I murmur on a much more real note, wanting to assuage any actual hesitancy she might have.

She nods, slowly grinding against my hand as I continue thrusting my fingers in and out of her. Without breaking my rhythm, I angle my hand so that my thumb can reach up and gently rub her clit in time with my pumps. A small, strangled sound escapes her, and her nails dig into the bare skin of my shoulders as she holds onto me for dear life.

"*Alec*," she pants, her eyebrows furrowing in agonized pleasure. "I need more."

"What do you need?" I taunt her.

"Alec," she whines, reaching down between us, reaching for my cock.

I maneuver my arm in her way, lowering my head and forcing her to meet my gaze. "Use your words, sweetheart," I murmur. "What do you want?"

She bites her lip, her chest heaving. "I want you inside of me," she relents.

Fuck. My cock jumps at her words, readier than ever. I smile. "Take off your swimsuit bottoms," I order, letting go of her so she can stand. She does as I say, removing her bikini bottoms and looping one of her arms through them so they won't float away.

"Legs back around my waist," I instruct, and I help her position herself back to where she was. It's easier than this type of position ever has been, since the water is basically doing all the work of holding her up.

I grip her hips, pulling her toward me, positioning my cock at her entrance. And then slowly, I slide inside.

The feeling is indescribable, and I sigh quietly at the pleasure that emulates from my core. Fuck, she feels good. Has any other woman felt this good? Surely they have, but I can't seem to remember any of them.

Ella must be feeling the same way because she grips my shoulders, moaning softly and closing her eyes. Holding tight to her hips, I use my hold on her body to create the leverage I need in order to thrust in and out of her. I do so slowly at first, reveling in the expression of pure ecstasy on Ella's face. And then I start pumping faster, my fingers digging into the flesh on Ella's hips as I practically slam her down onto me over and over again.

She cries out softly, obviously trying to keep her voice down. "Shhhh, sweetheart," I remind her. I'd cover her mouth like last time if I didn't need to keep hold of her like this.

I pump faster, feeling my pleasure building and building. But I want Ella to come first. I need her to.

"Touch yourself," I demand in between thrusts.

She opens her eyes, looking at me quizzically.

"Touch yourself," I repeat. "Your breasts, your clit, whatever's going to make you cum." I'd do it myself if I had a free hand.

She hesitates for just a second before obeying, keeping one hand on my shoulder to steady herself while one ventures beneath the water, between her legs.

"Good girl," I praise, and that same spark of desire lights in her eyes.

I watch her expression closely as I continue thrusting. She closes her eyes, her moans becoming more and more high pitched. She bobs in the water as I thrust in and out of her, the bare tips of her breasts— exposed from when I'd pulled down her bikini top earlier, and only propped up by the fabric bunched beneath them—breaking the surface again and again, pink and erect.

Her expression hardens, looking almost pained, and with a final cry, I can see her climax rushing though her, her pussy clenching around my cock. It's then that I let myself go, letting the ecstasy wash over me as I empty myself inside of her.

Ella collapses against me, wrapping her arms around my neck and resting her head on my shoulder. I breathe heavily, panting for air. I glance around. I can see the others haven't moved from where they were just a few minutes ago, and none are looking in our direction. No one knows what just happened between us.

Or that it's going to continue happening if I have anything to do with it.

After a few seconds, Ella unwraps herself from around me, hopping back down to the ocean floor. She shoots me one of those adorably shy smiles while she repositions her bikini top and slides on her bottoms.

"I'm kind of hungry," she says. "How about we go track down some lunch?"

I grin. "Anything for the wife."

Chapter 14

Ella

I lay on a beach towel, soaking up the sun, my toes wiggling in the sand. I sip from a can of coke, glancing over at Alec and his brothers as they play some sort of beach volleyball game—whatever game a group of three can come up with. So far, it's including some shouting and laughing hysterically—at least on Aiden's part.

Marcus and Julia are off strolling the beach hand in hand, which leaves Olivia, Lilly, and I to sunbathe in the loungers and on beach towels.

"Want some peach slices?" Lilly offers from beside me.

I sit up, reaching over to grab a few peach slices from the Tupperware container she's holding out. "Thanks," I say.

"You and Alec seem to be getting along well," Lilly comments. Her expression is one I can't quite read. She's smiling, but it seems mischievous.

I freeze, immediately thinking back to what we'd done barely an hour ago. Had they noticed? Did they *know* what we did? I can feel myself growing red just thinking about it. Shit. I'm sure she and Olivia are at least noticing that.

Lilly chuckles. "Don't freak out," she says softly. "It just seems like Alec really likes you."

"Well, we're supposed to act like we like each other," I say casually. Which is true. But I wonder if everyone else has sensed the shift since last night.

"I've known Alec for a few years," Olivia chimes in. "And I know when he's being genuine or not."

I pretend to busy myself with taking a sip of Coca-Cola, processing her words. Could Alec actually *like* me? Do *I* like *him*? The last twenty-four hours has been a complete and utter whirlwind. I went from hating the guy to letting him fuck my brains out.

And I want to let him do it again.

I bite my lip. "You think he actually likes me?"

"He definitely likes you as a person. Which is, in itself, a hard thing to accomplish when it comes to Alec," Lilly says with a laugh.

"But there's also something else I'm picking up on," Olivia adds. She tilts her head, then shrugs. "I don't know. Vibes."

I snort. Vibes. Yes, there have definitely been *vibes*.

"What kind of person does he normally date?" I find myself asking, genuinely curious.

Olivia tilts her head again. "Honestly, he doesn't date a whole lot."

"At all?" I question.

She shakes her head. "Not that I know of. Asher said he had a pretty serious relationship years ago but that it ended badly."

I raise my eyebrows.

"Says he was cheated on and then never really got back out there," Olivia finishes.

"That's awful," I say.

Both Olivia and Lilly nod.

"If you ask me, he's due for a relationship," Lilly says. "A real one." She gives me another look that I can't quite decipher. Is that hope I see in there? Is she suggesting that this fake marriage of ours could somehow turn real? But there's no way. No way Alec would want a wife like me. Sure, I can play the part, but I'm decidedly *not* the part. And there's a difference.

Suddenly frustrated by this new train of thought, I turn away, flipping over on the beach towel and lying on my stomach. Olivia and Lilly fall into conversation beside me, mentioning shops in town they want to explore before heading back on the boat later today.

I press the side of my face against the beach towel and close my eyes, feeling the soft rays of sun soaking into my back. I take a deep breath, pushing all thoughts out of my head and trying my hardest not to think about Alec King.

Chapter 15

Ella

At the end of the day, the group of us saunters back on the boat, sun kissed and happily exhausted from a day on the beach. We eat dinner, sit around on the deck as the sun sets, sipping drinks and chatting, and two by two, each of the couples retire to their rooms as the night wears on.

Aiden and Lilly are the last to leave us, Aiden finishing his last drink and setting the empty glass on the table. "That's it for me tonight," he says, glancing sideways at Lilly, who shoots him a look that says she agrees.

They stand, pushing their chairs back.

"Goodnight, guys," Alec says. "See you in the morning."

"Goodnight," I call as the two of them head off, Aiden's arm slung around Lilly's shoulder.

The lights from the dock glisten off the dark water below. Alec and I are left in nothing but the dim glow of the lights inside the cabin. The breeze on the deck is cool, ruffling my hair as I stare out at the vast darkness of the ocean.

"Did you have a good day?" Alec asks quietly from beside me.

"Yeah," I reply with a smile, turning to meet his gaze. "It was a great day." We hold eye contact for just a second longer than necessary, and I know what we're both thinking about.

I clear my throat, looking back out at the ocean. "So do you think that this merger with Marcus is still going to happen?" I ask.

"Almost a hundred percent," Alec answers. "I mean, the odds were already pretty high, but after these last few days, I think everyone is hitting it off incredibly well."

I nod in agreement. "Strange way to do business," I say with a laugh. "Cruising through the Caribbean." I take a sip of my drink.

Alec chuckles. "Well, that's how the rich get things done."

I raise my eyebrows. "Ah, the *rich*."

He snorts. "Having not come from money, I still find myself mocking the whole culture."

"Oh, it's very mockable," I agree, nodding. "Like the amount of money you pay me just to walk your dog. I'm not complaining, just observing," I tease, smirking.

He laughs.

"Oh, and the amount you're paying me to sit here right now and have this conversation with you." I lean back in my chair and take a long, theatrical drink from my glass, maintaining eye contact with him over the rim.

He smirks. "And what are your plans for this ridiculous sum?" he asks me.

I make a show of thinking long and hard. "Vet school," I answer honestly.

He raises a brow, intrigued. "You want to become a vet," he says.

I nod, pulling my knees up against my chest and resting my feet on the chair, settling in. "I've always wanted to be a vet. I graduated with my degree in Animal Sciences back in May, and I've been saving up a bit before applying to vet school."

Alec nods slowly, gazing at me. "You'd be a good vet," he finally decides.

I smile. "Thanks. I love animals, so it always seemed like a good fit."

"So you'll use the money to pay for vet school," he says.

I shrug. "Part of it, at least. School is expensive, so it probably won't cover it all, but it will decrease my loan amount substantially."

He stares at me for a long moment before looking off at the water and taking a sip of his drink.

"And what about you?" I bring the conversation back to him. "This merger the achievement of your dreams? It's hard to imagine going up from here," I comment.

The ghost of a smile plays on his lips. "That's the problem with making it big. You suddenly run out of places to go." He says it in a light tone, but the words somehow feel heavy.

I bite my lip, thinking. "Is it everything you wanted it to be?" I finally ask.

He hesitates. "Almost." The word is uttered quietly, almost a whisper.

His gaze still glued to mine, we sit there for a heartbeat in silence. "Well, almost is better than nothing," I finally answer.

He smiles. "True."

I break our gaze to stare out at the water once more. Not because there's anything to look at, but mainly to remove myself from his hypnotic stare. But when I turn back, he's still looking at me.

"What?" I find myself asking with a shy giggle.

He cocks his head. "You're just not what I thought you'd be like. The real you."

I raise an eyebrow. "What, smart? Interesting?"

He rolls his eyes. "No. I'm not surprised by that. I guess I'm surprised by how much I enjoy being around you. So maybe it's *me* I'm surprised at."

"You know, I'm surprised by that as well," I admit.

It's his turn to feign offense. "You thought I'd be too stuck up to be fun?"

"Oh, that's exactly what I thought," I say with a devilish grin.

He laughs, throwing his head back. "I guess I deserve that."

He leans forward in his chair, and the movement causes his knee to rest against mine. The touch is electric, and my gaze darts to where our bodies connect. I find myself leaning toward him, and Alec spans the final distance between us, pressing his lips softly against mine. The kiss is slow, unhurried—much like our other kisses—but it somehow makes it that much more sensual. Butterflies flitter through my stomach. He pulls away, resting his forehead against mine momentarily. His gaze darkens, a glint in them.

Suddenly he stands, pulling me to my feet after him and then back into the boat. I know where his destination is, and I know what's on his mind. Because it's on my mind as well.

We make it back to the room, and his hands are all over my body the second we step inside, barely having time to close the door behind us. He presses me against the wall, kissing me hungrily as his hands work on the buttons of my shirt. Without breaking our kiss, he slides my shirt over my shoulders, tossing it to the ground. He reaches behind me to unclasp my bra, and once my breasts are free, his hands are immediately all over them.

I moan into his mouth as he gropes my breasts, squeezing roughly and thumbing my nipples. He moves to unbutton my shorts, breaking our kiss to demand, "Step out of these. Your underwear too."

Despite the fact that he's still fully clothed, I find myself doing what he says. Something about how he bosses me around has me wanting to obey his every whim.

I slide my shorts off, then my panties, and I'm standing before him completely nude. He scans my body, his eyes lingering hungrily on my breasts and pussy.

I reach for his shirt, starting to undo the buttons, but he turns around, pulling me with him toward the bed. He leads me onto it, then lies down. I begin to straddle him, but he stops me. I stare down at him, puzzled.

He smirks. "Up here," he instructs, gesturing to his face.

It takes just a second, but understanding finally washes over me, and I feel my face grow red. "You want me to …"

He nods.

"But I've—never done that," I stammer.

His eyebrow quirks up. "All the more reason to do it right now."

Self conscious, I hesitate. I've never had a man eat me out that way before. It's always felt so … in your face. Literally.

Alec reaches for my hand, tugging me toward him. "Let me make you feel good, Ella," he says, and while he's asking me to sit on his face, he still seems to regain all the control here.

Summoning my courage, I do as he says, crawling up the bed, lifting my knee, and hovering over his face. I stare down at him, hesitant to lower myself, even though it's borderline humiliating knowing that he's getting a pretty intimate view of all of me.

"Hold the bedframe if you need to," he says.

I reach for the metal frame of the bed in front of me.

"Now sit down."

"But I—"

"Sit down, Ella, or I'll make you."

I slowly lower myself, hovering just over his face, and as if he can't wait any longer, Alec reaches up, grabbing my waist and pulling me down on top of him. I gasp as his tongue comes into contact with my center, sliding along my slit. He slowly runs his tongue back and forth, back and forth, and then he inserts his tongue inside of me.

I throw my head back, sighing. Fuck, this feels good.

He goes back to sliding his tongue along my slit, and when he reaches my clit, I moan, gripping the bedframe. His tongue draws slow, deliberate circles around my clit, causing embarrassingly hysterical noises to come out of my mouth. My hips move of their own accord, grinding against him, and he digs his fingers into my upper thighs to hold me still.

He picks up speed, and I grip the bedframe for dear life, leaning forward, my breasts dangling below me as I rock my hips against him, moaning.

"Oh, *god*," I whine as the pleasure builds within me. Any leftover dignity or embarrassment leaves me as I succumb to the pleasure of what Alec is doing to me, desperate for release. I grind against him as the pressure builds, moaning deeply and unable to stop myself.

My orgasm crashes through me, and I cry out, shuddering as the waves roll through me. I crawl off of Alec and collapse on the bed beside him, my chest heaving.

Propping himself up on his elbow, he grins down at me, drawing a lazy finger from my collarbone in between my breasts. "Was that good?" he asks me.

I turn my head to face him. "Yeah," I pant. "Yeah, it was good."

I eye him up and down. He's still fully clothed, but I plan to change that. I sit up on my knees, reaching for his shirt, beginning to unbutton it. Alec smiles up at me and joins in. When I get to his pants, he shuffles off the bed, pulling his pants down and stepping out them, doing the same with his underwear. And there he stands, fully nude.

I get off the bed and stride toward him, aware of how his gaze slowly slides along my body. I reach him, running my hands over his chest, his muscles flexing under my touch, and then I slide to my knees in front of him.

I take his cock in my hand, stroking it a few times, and then, looking up to meet his gaze as I do it, I slowly lick from the bottom of his shaft up to the tip.

His mouth drops open, and a quiet sigh escapes him.

I do it again, licking along his shaft, and then swirling my tongue at the tip of his cock. He closes his mouth, and I can see him working his jaw, his eyes darkening. And when I slide his cock into my mouth, he loses his composure, closing his eyes and moaning.

A flurry of arousal flickers in my lower belly as I slowly pump my mouth along his shaft, taking his cock as deep as I can. His fingers tangle in my hair, pulling so hard it almost hurts.

I moan softly as I suck at his cock, pumping my mouth along his shaft.

"Fuck, Ella," he chokes out. I feel his cock pulse in my mouth. "I'm going to cum," he groans, gripping my hair harder.

I moan in response, pumping faster. And then with a sigh, he finishes, emptying his liquid inside of me. I do my best to swallow, and Alec pulls out of me.

He stares down at me, a satiated grin on his face. He reaches down to thumb away some mess on the side of my lip. "That's my good girl," he murmurs.

Chapter 16

Ella

We set sail for Florida the next morning with plans to arrive at port the morning after, meaning today is our last day of vacation. My last day in the Caribbean. Maybe forever. Who knows when I'd ever be back here?

I'd woken up early this morning when I'd felt the boat taking off, leaving a sleeping Alec to go above deck and watch as we left the Bahamas behind. Now I'm sitting on the deck with a cup of coffee, leaning back in a lounge chair as I watch the early morning light dancing across the water.

"This seat taken?" a voice pulls me from my thoughts.

I look over my shoulder to see Julia, her hair pulled back into a low bun and a bright smile across her face. "Not at all," I say, returning her grin. "Please." I gesture to the seat beside me.

She sits down with a cup of coffee of her own, settling in. We sit in amicable silence for a moment. "So, how did you like the trip?" she asks me.

"Oh, it was incredible," I gush. "I've never seen water like this in my life." *And maybe never again,* I make sure to omit.

Julia nods. "The Bahamas are my absolute favorite islands to visit," she says. "Just gorgeous."

"Have you been to many others in the Caribbean?" I ask.

"Oh, yes. Probably most of them. Aruba, Turks and Caicos, Jamaica. But the Bahamas has my heart."

"I'd love to go to all those places," I comment.

"Well, why don't you? Does Alec not take you anywhere?" Julia asks with a laugh.

I know she's only kidding, but suddenly I'm realizing how problematic this could be to our story. She's right. If I truly was Alec's wife, I would most likely be more well-traveled. "Oh—well, we're planning more trips soon, we just haven't gotten around to it," I lie.

Julia raises an eyebrow. "Oh, where are thinking?"

"Europe," I lie, spouting the first place that comes to mind.

"Anywhere specific?" she presses.

"Spain. And England. France too," I say.

"Beautiful countries," she says with a shake of her head.

"You've been?" I ask.

"Many times."

A silence settles around us as we sip our coffees and stare out at the turquoise ocean. "How long have you known Alec?" Julia asks.

I startle at the question. "Um …" I begin, thinking back to our story. "Only about a year. It was quite the whirlwind romance."

She nods, looking at me. "A whole year," she repeats.

Nerves tighten in my belly. I nod. "Yeah. Crazy how so much can change in just a year."

She smiles, breaking our gaze and staring back out at the ocean. "You're not really married, are you?"

"What?" I stutter. How did she …? I panic. "Of course we're married," I press. "We got married last summer."

She turns to meet my gaze, but instead of an accusatory stare like I'd anticipated, there's nothing but warmth. "Sweetheart, I know when people are married, when people are comfortable around each other—and you two most certainly aren't."

I feel like I've been punched in the gut. Shit. I thought we'd been doing so well. The trip is practically over, and I thought we'd accomplished our mission. I shake my head. "I … how could you tell?" I finally whisper.

She smiles. "You're an unlikely match, for starters. And you're much too excited and blown away by the niceties that a wife of Alec King would be used to. But the real thing that gave it away is that you don't have that comfortable, loving cadence that a husband and wife had."

I frown. Seriously? I thought we'd acted the part. Especially considering that the last few days Alec and I have been definitely acting like a husband and a wife behind closed doors.

"You have the cadence of two people who are in love but are afraid to tell each other," she finishes.

I feel the color drain from my face. "What?" The word floats out of my mouth on a whisper, barely spoken.

Julia leans toward me, resting her hand on mine. "Sweetheart, whatever is going on between you and Alec King, you need to speak your truth."

"But I … there isn't anything to say," I reply with a shake of my head.

Julia smiles in amusement. "From my vantage point, there's a whole lot that needs to be said. From both of you."

I stare out at the ocean, every nerve in my body on fire. If Julia could so easily see through us, can everyone else? Does Marcus know this was a sham too? Do Alec's brothers know there's more going on than just pretend? "Will this interfere with the merger?" I ask quietly.

At this, Julia chuckles. "Oh, Marcus is completely oblivious to all this. And I'm certainly not going to tell him. This is between you and Alec, and the merger is between the King boys and my husband—two completely sperate things, in my book."

Relief settles over me.

"I just thought you'd benefit from some motherly advice."

At this, I turn to her, taking in the warmth of her smile, and I smile back.

"And that advice is to tell Alec how you feel. Too much is left unsaid in this world. Don't add your feelings to that list." She glances down at her mug of coffee. "Time for a refill," she says, standing and sauntering back into the cabin, leaving me alone to process the feelings I've been too afraid to face until now.

Chapter 17

Ella

I end up spending the majority of the day with Olivia and Lilly, lounging by the pool and soaking up the sun. The guys join us in the afternoon, and while part of me wants to reveal my conversation with Julia to Alec, I feel like I can't in front of everyone. Besides, it was pretty private, and if I told him part of it, I'd have to tell him all of it. And *all* of it includes my feelings. And I'm not even sure what those are yet. So maybe it's best to keep it to myself. And Julia promised not to tell Marcus and that it wouldn't affect the merger, so there's no harm done.

"Damn, I'm feeling the drinks from last night," Aiden moans, hiding his eyes from the sun with his forearm.

Lilly laughs.

"How are you not hungover?" he asks her.

"I chug water when I drink. You should try it," she replies.

"Aren't we a bit old to be getting drunk?" Alec asks.

"Maybe *you* are," Aiden shoots back, to which Alec flashes him a middle finger. "Olivia, have you been drunk at least once this trip?" He turns his attention to her. "Have you been drinking at all?"

She rolls her eyes.

"Come on, this is what vacations are for," he says. "And you too, Asher. What the hell? Normally you're the life of the party."

Asher smirks, then shoots a sidelong glance at Olivia. She smirks back but says nothing.

Alec straightens on the lounger he's sitting on. "What was that look?" he says with a cocked brow.

Asher and Olivia exchange another look, and at this point, all of us are fully engaged. Olivia laughs, shrugging. "Well, we weren't going to say anything for another week or so, but …" She smiles at Asher. "That 'party' you spoke of is about to get a bit bigger."

Lilly's mouth drops open, and Alec grins. I clasp my hands over my mouth in delighted shock. It takes Aiden a second longer to fully comprehend. "What?" he asks, glancing between Olivia and Asher.

"We're having a baby," Asher clarifies with a laugh.

"Holy shit!" Aiden yells, jumping up and crossing the deck. He leans down to pull Olivia into a hug, and then turns and gives one to Asher.

"Congratulations, you guys," Alec says. "That's incredible."

"We're really excited," Olivia says with a huge grin.

Aiden returns to his spot next to Lilly, pulling her in for a side hug. I glance to Alec, but he isn't looking at me. Instead, his gaze is pinned on Asher and Olivia. How the two of them are gazing at each other, full of excitement and love. The way Asher puts his hand on Olivia's back, rubbing gently. Is that … sadness I see in Alec's eyes. Longing? For the first time, I wonder how this week has been for him. To be around three loving couples—two of them his brothers—and not have that for himself. Has it been hard? I feel selfish for only considering it now. Because while Alec and I have spent some steamy moments together, that's certainly not love. Right?

My mind flits back to what Julia had told me this morning. How she could tell there was something there. And while she might be right on my end, I have no idea what's going on in Alec's mind.

We dock at the port early the next morning, and I'm awoken by Alec quietly gathering his stuff up in his suitcase. We'd spent last night in bed together, and this morning, as he gets up, leaving his side cold and empty, I wonder if I'll ever find myself lying next to him again. But I quickly shove the thought from my mind as I get up as well and begin getting ready.

Half an hour later, we're all up in the main cabin with our suitcases and belongings, saying our goodbyes to Marcus and Julia.

"This was such a wonderful time," Marcus says. "So glad you all could join us. We'll be in touch about the company logistics early next week," he assures the guys.

Julia catches my eye as we're leaving the boat, reaching out to brush a reassuring hand across my arm. "Good luck," she says quietly, and I simply smile and nod.

The flight back to Seattle is uneventful. Tired from the trip, most of us either end up napping or on our phones. I wish there was a truly private place for

Alec and I to talk, but there isn't. When we land, I say my goodbyes to everyone.

"It was so nice to meet you, Ella," Olivia says.

"Good luck with vet school," Lilly wishes me.

The guys wish me luck as well, and then Alec and I head to his car. I glance at him surreptitiously as he starts the car, an awkwardness settling over us. Because now …

Now that the vacation is over, now that the mission was completed, the merger is on … what are we?

Had you asked me this question before the vacation, I'd have told you we would be nothing. We'd go back to the way things were before and never speak of this, and I'd be a hundred grand richer. But now? After everything that's happened? It feels wrong to say we're nothing. But it feels terrifying to say we're not.

Alec drives me to my apartment in silence, and that silence becomes more and more suffocating the closer we get. He parks outside my building and helps me carry my things up the steps and to my front door. We stop in front of it, awkwardly shuffling.

It's then that he offers me a small smile. "We did it," he says quietly. "Thank you, again. I mean it. You really saved me by doing this."

I nod, staring up at him. And while I want to end this like it was nothing more than a transactional relationship, I can't help but think about Julia and what she said.

"Yeah," I say instead. "It was fun." I want desperately to ask him what we are now. If there will be more, or if everything was just a fling, but the nerves in my stomach stop me. "Oh," I say, looking down at the diamond ring on my finger. I pull it off. "I should give this back to you."

He shakes his head. "Keep it. Consider it a part of the deal. You can wear it or sell it or keep it as a memento."

I raise my eyebrows. "An expensive memento," I comment.

He shrugs. "You earned it."

I know he means it to sound kind, but something about it sits uncomfortably inside me. I bite my lip. Is he going to say anything more? Address what went down between us? Or was it all simply nothing to him?

"I'll see you next week?" he says.

"Next week?" I echo.

"When you come to walk Betty."

"Oh. Betty. Yes. I'll see you then," I reply.

He shoots me one last smile before turning on his heel and walking back down the steps and to his car. I watch him go in silence, trying to ignore the sinking feeling of disappointment in my stomach. I unlock my door and step inside, immediately greeted by an ecstatic Howard.

I kneel on the floor, grabbing his wiggling body into a hug and letting my tears dissolve in his fur.

Chapter 18

Alec

"Sounds great, Marcus," Asher says, leaning over the phone. "I'll have my assistant touch base with yours to finalize the contracts."

"Sounds good, boys," Marcus's voice says from the speaker phone.

Aiden and I say our goodbyes, and Asher hangs up the phone, letting his excitement explode with a punch to the air. "Hell, yeah!" he says.

The three of us take turns high-fiving and practically jumping for joy.

"I can't believe it," Aiden says with a shake of his head, a stupid grin on his face. "We did it!"

"We did it," I repeat, pulling him in for a hug.

"I have to call Olivia," Asher says, picking up his phone. "She's gonna be so excited." He dials her number and puts his phone to his ear, heading out of the office.

Aiden and I remain, still grinning at each other like kids. "Man, did you ever think our company would come to something like this?" he asks me.

I shake my head, laughing. "Never."

Aiden pulls out his phone, obviously texting someone. "Who you texting?" I ask.

"Lilly," he answers without looking up. "Want to share the good news."

I smile, but I can't help the small tug at my heart knowing that there isn't anyone *I* want to share the good news with. It's that same tug I'd felt when Asher and Olivia had announced her pregnancy on the boat. Not jealousy, per se. I mean, I'm elated for them both. And I get to be an uncle. That part hasn't really sunk in yet. But at thirty-seven, shouldn't I be on my way toward that as well? I'm not necessarily ready for a kid, but shouldn't I at least know who I'd be having kids with? Will I ever have that? A family? A wife and kids? It never really seemed important to me until right now.

I suddenly notice that a long pause has amassed between Aiden and I. He's looking at me funny. "How's Ella?" he asks.

I frown. "Fine, I assume," I answer. "I sent her the money yesterday."

Aiden snorts. "Not what I meant."

I raise an eyebrow. "What did you mean?"

Aiden shakes his head. "You haven't seen her since the trip?"

It's only been a few days. While she came by to walk Betty yesterday, I was at work. In fact, I made sure I was at work, but I'm not going to tell Aiden that. "Why would we talk?"

Aiden makes a face at me. "You're not serious."

I make a face right back at him.

"Come on, man. You are the most obtuse guy I know."

"Aiden, just say what you wanna say," I snap, suddenly growing irritated by this conversation. Although why, I'm not sure. Aiden's teasing has never truly bothered me before.

"Why aren't you dating her?" he asks me.

"Dating?" I repeat. "I hired her for a job, and she did that job."

"And you spent the entire trip making goo-goo eyes at her. And she made goo-goo eyes back, by the way."

"Doesn't mean we should date."

"Why not?"

"It's inappropriate." It's the truest thing I've said in this conversation. Because as much as I might want to date Ella, it's not appropriate. None of this entire situation was appropriate, so I should really distance myself from it as much as possible.

Because if I'm honest with myself, I regret what happened. I regret giving into my desires and doing what I did with Ella. It had been the best week of my life, but deep down, I know it wasn't fair to her. It had been a monumental abuse of power. I'd hired her to do a job. A job that I'd assured her wouldn't include anything inappropriate. And then we went ahead and did that anyway. And it's all my fault. And to act on my continuing desires and try to make this relationship go further? I don't know how she feels. It could make her uncomfortable, make her feel used, and worst—endanger her job. I'd hate to have her quit and lose business all because I couldn't keep my emotions in check.

No, as much as I like Ella—as much as I'm obsessed with her and find my nights consumed by visions of her—I can't act on it.

Aiden sighs but doesn't respond. And if I know anything about Aiden, he's silent when he knows I'm right but doesn't want to admit defeat.

"I don't know, man," he finally says. "Your relationship with her was already toeing the line. I don't think there's any harm in telling her how you feel. The worst she can say is no, and knowing you, if she did, you'd respect that." He chuckles. "But I doubt she'd say no."

I roll my eyes, standing from the desk. "Doesn't matter. What matters now is going out for celebratory drinks because we just closed the deal of a lifetime," I say with a grin. "Let's go find Asher."

At the mention of drinks, Aiden concedes, and we head off to find our brother.

Chapter 19

Ella

I stare in utter shock at the amount showing up in my mobile banking app. $100,987. My jack is slack just taking in the numbers. Holy. Fucking. Shit.

A laugh bubbles up my throat, and I can't even stop it. I think back to last week when I'd forlornly looked out at the Caribbean Ocean, sure I'd never see it again. Maybe I could spare a bit of this vet school money and take myself on another vacation. Surely that wouldn't be too irresponsible, would it? Julia had said Aruba was nice.

And while the high from this money is definitely coursing through my veins, I can't help but think back to last week a bit sadly.

I haven't seen Alec since. I've been by to walk Betty a handful of times, but each time, he isn't there. Which isn't wholly unusual, but I thought we'd speak at least a little.

I feel stupid just thinking about it. What was I expecting? That this handsome, rich, successful man would fall madly in love with me and want more than just a mere few days of hooking up? *He held up his end of the deal,* Ella, I remind myself. *You pretended to be his wife. He paid you. It's over now.*

Julia's words of wisdom are fading as the days pass by. It doesn't matter what she thought she saw. If Alec was interested, he'd have acted interested by now. It's not complicated.

If only I could make my heart understand that.

I reach down to pop a kiss onto Howard's head before grabbing my keys and heading for the door. I decide that tonight is celebratory, so I'll be splurging on high end sushi, and I'll grab a bone for Howard too.

But first, I need to walk Betty. I feel bad that walking her now fills me with dread. It's not Betty's fault. She's a sweetheart. If only her owner wasn't so complicated.

I tug my jacket tight around my body as I walk from my place to Alec's, missing the warm Caribbean sun.

When I enter the building, I take the elevator to the top floor and unlock the door to Alec's apartment. I step inside and am immediately greeted by an excited Betty, jumping up and down and whining.

"Hi there, girl," I say, leaning down to fix her leash. "Ready for a nice walk?"

I take Betty outside, and together we stroll through the neighborhoods. The drizzle seems to be letting up a bit today, which I'm happy about. I can't wait for actual spring to arrive, when the cherry trees blossom and flowers litter every side street.

After a long and satisfying walk, I bring Betty back to the apartment. I walk in, unclasping Betty's leash and turning to hang it on the hook by the doorway. It's then that I feel a presence in the room, and I turn to see Alec looking just as surprised as I feel.

"Hey," I say softly. I don't know why I'm surprised. It's his home, after all.

"Hi," he answers. He stands from a barstool at the kitchen counter where he'd been sitting, walking over to me. "How have you been?" He seems to ask the question genuinely, but there's a tension in the air, as if he's unsure how to act. Which, to be fair, I am too. I spent the last week pretending to be his wife.

And sleeping in his bed.

And now … we're just back to normal?

It feels so weird and terrible and … wrong.

"Good," I lie. "I got your deposit. Thank you."

He nods. "Glad it went through okay."

I force a smile.

We stand in awkward silence for a moment, the seconds becoming more and more unbearable as they pass. Seeing him again, my heart feels like it's about to break in two. I didn't know it would feel this terrible to be face to face with him again, but it hurts more than I can bear.

I bite my lip, looking away. How can he just act like nothing happened between us? Was it *actually* nothing to him? The realization crashes over me like a ton of bricks. Fuck. I should've known. He's probably used to getting whatever girl he wants. Last week was just fun to him. Nothing more. How could I have been so stupid to think otherwise?

And I realize I was holding onto the tiniest shred of hope that once I saw him again, things would be different. I'd see that familiar spark in his eye, that smile, something to tell me that what I felt was reciprocated.

But now I know it was all just as fake as our marriage.

"Um …" I start, staring down at my feet. "I think you should probably find a new dog walker," I force myself to say.

He looks shocked. "What? Are you starting vet school?" Hope flickers across his face.

I shrug. "Soon, probably. So I should start offloading some of my clients."

He frowns slightly. "Why don't you keep doing it until you start school? That way you can keep saving up."

"Just—" I snap but stop myself. "I said you should find a new dog walker. So you should." I turn to go, but Alec strides across the room, reaching for my arm. His touch sends an electric current through me, and I pull away.

"Is something wrong, Ella?" he asks, looking down at me in concern.

I shake my head. "Nothing's wrong."

I try to continue, but he stands in my way. "You're lying. Tell me what it is."

"Alec, move," I plead.

"What's wrong?" he repeats, his frown deepening.

"Everything!" I snap. "I—I …" I shake my head, sighing in frustration. "I thought that after last week, after everything that happened, that you … *cared*. About me." I look up to meet his gaze. "But it turns out you basically just paid me to be your wife *and* prostitute for the week."

Shock washes over his features. "Ella, *no*. I never meant for that—for any of that to happen."

"Of course you didn't," I mutter. "You never meant to get involved with me. I wasn't even your first choice to play your wife—it just happened. Even Julia could tell I was wrong for the part." I'm rambling now, but I can't stop myself.

"Julia?" Alec repeats.

"She talked to me the last day of the cruise. She said she knew we weren't really married. Don't worry, Marcus doesn't know, and she promised she wouldn't tell."

"She saw through us?" he asks quietly.

"She did. And she also thought something was there, but she was obviously wrong about that too. Just like me." I shake my head. "I should never have allowed myself to get caught up in all this. Your *real* wife would never be someone like me."

I brush past him toward the door, and this time he doesn't stop me, seemingly too shocked to even move. I hurry through the door, slamming it behind me.

Chapter 20

Ella

Eating sushi alone that night, however good it is, is a bit of a bummer. At least Howard's face lights up in excitement when I give him his bone. Alec tries to call me the next day, but I don't answer. And he doesn't text or call again, so I can only assume his apology would probably have been half-assed. All he wants is to rid himself of his guilt, probably. He toyed with a younger girl and hurt her, and now he feels bad.

Well, welcome to the club, asshole.

I spend the rest of the week trying to rid him from my mind. I stop walking Betty, which I feel slightly bad about knowing that she'll probably miss me, but I already told Alec about it, and I need the space. I stuff all of the clothes he'd given me, and the ring, into a box and shove it under the bed. I don't want to throw it away. At the very least, they're worth an insane amount of money—but I can't stand to see them right now. Maybe in a few months, I'll feel differently.

It's Friday night, and I'm wrapped up in a blanket on my couch watching a movie, with Howard resting his head on my leg, fast asleep. I'd spent the last few hours compiling my vet school application, and I'm finally ready to submit it. I want to sleep it on, go over it again in the morning, and then send it off. However unfairly Alec may have treated me, I do have to admit that the financial boost really gave me the motivation to take the jump and apply. I'm ready. And I'm excited.

A sound at the front door has Howard sitting up, suddenly awake and fully alert. I hear a knock, and Howard is leaping to the floor, barking manically.

"Shhhh," I chide him, getting up and heading to the door. I swing it open, expecting a mistaken food delivery—unit 103 packages often accidentally end up here—but am shocked to find myself face to face with none other than Alec King.

I freeze, my eyes going wide. He stares back at me. He looks ... nervous? "Alec," I say. It's the only word I can summon.

"Ella," he says. "Can I come in?"

"Um, sure." I step aside so he can enter. Howard jumps up and down in excitement, and Alec pats his head in greeting.

I follow him into the living room where he turns around. I wait for him to explain his presence here, my hands crossed across my chest. "If this is about walking Betty—" I start.

"No, no it's not about that."

I nod. "Okay."

"I ..." He stares down at his hands. "I felt like I needed to apologize."

And there it is. Just like I thought. He only wants to assuage his guilt. Although I suppose an apology is better than nothing. I continue to keep my arms folded across my chest, saying nothing.

"I shouldn't have let anything happen between us," he says. "I should have kept the relationship professional. Like I promised. That's on me, and I'm sorry." He meets my gaze, his eyes pleading for forgiveness. Although I'm not sure I'm ready to give it.

"Let?" I echo. "As if you should have stopped me? Like I was the moving force in all this?"

He shakes his head. "No, not you. I shouldn't have let *myself* give in to my desires—my feelings for you."

Feelings. The word catches in my brain and sticks.

"And regardless of how I felt—how I feel—it's not fair to you. I didn't, and don't, want you to feel obligated. As if the more intimate part of our relationship was wrapped up in the deal. The lines blurred, and I'm afraid I took advantage of that."

I cock my head. What is he saying? "What *do* you feel, Alec?" I ask bluntly.

He stares at me for a long moment. "I feel …" He trails off and then sighs. "You're the only woman in a long, long time who has ever made me feel excited to wake up in the morning, excited to see you, and excited to see where … everything could go. And I've spent every day apart from you this last week wishing you were next to me. Wishing we were back on that boat." He takes a deep breath. "But putting those expectations on you isn't fair."

"Isn't fair?" I reply. "You're making that decision for me. What's fair about that? Have you wondered how *I* feel?"

He's quiet for a moment, seemingly surprised.

"I've spent the entire week furious with you because I thought you used me for nothing more than a plaything. That you slept with me just for fun and abandoned me when it was over."

He shakes his head. "Ella, I—"

"I spent last week with you on the boat falling for someone I never thought I would, seeing sides of you I admire, adore, and—thinking maybe, just maybe, there could be a future there."

A mixture of emotions wash over Alec's face. Shock, happiness, relief, and some emotions I can't quite identify. "You mean that?" he finally asks. "You're not just saying it?"

I throw my hands up, shaking my head. "Why would I embarrass myself like this if I didn't mean it?" I say, my voice suddenly catching in my throat.

"Ella." He spans the distance between us, taking my hand in his and reaching his other up to cup my face. He smiles. "This is the least embarrassing thing I've ever heard. In fact, it might just be the best thing I've ever heard."

I grin up at him hesitantly. "The best thing? So does that mean you feel the same?"

He rolls his eyes with small laugh. "Didn't I already say that?"

Unable to stop myself, I reach for his tie, pulling him down toward me and pressing my lips firmly against his. He responds in kind, kissing me back desperately and then grabbing my upper thighs and hoisting me up until my legs are wrapped around his waist. I throw my arms around his neck, tangling my fingers in his hair.

Our kiss deepens, Alec's tongue sliding between my lips and tangling with my own. He walks forward until my back hits the nearest wall, pressing me up against it and kissing me harder. Pinning me against the wall with his hips, he uses his free hand to grasp the hem of my t-shirt, breaking our kiss just long enough to pull it over my head.

Having been simply lounging at home, I'm not wearing a bra underneath, much to Alec's delighted surprise. He hoists me higher up the wall, holding me up with hands under my ass as he leans down to take one of my nipples into his mouth. I moan, clinging to him as he takes his time sucking one breast, then the other, flicking my nipples with his tongue and nibbling softly. I tangle my fingers in his hair, desperate for more.

Suddenly he puts me down, and before I can say anything, he spins me around, pulling my body back against his. I can feel his arousal against my backside, full and apparent. He spends his time fondling my breasts, squeezing and pinching until I'm a whimpering mess, and then his hand travels south, under the waistband of my sweatpants and below my panties.

"God, Ella, you're so wet for me," he breathes in my ear.

I practically melt. I buck my hips as he slides a teasing finger along my slit. "Please, Alec," I beg, desperate. He responds by inserting a finger inside of my aching pussy, and I moan, leaning my head back against his chest and closing my eyes. He gently massages my breast with one hand while pumping a finger in and out of me with his other, while my hushed cries fill the room.

All of a sudden, he stops, pulling out of me. I cry out softly in surprise, but before I can react, he's grabbed the waistband of my sweatpants and panties and slides them down in one smooth motion. I hear the fumbling of his belt buckle and his pants unzipping. Then he pushes me against the wall. I gasp.

"Spread your legs for me, sweetheart," he requests, and I do as he says, my face and chest pressed against the wall.

He grips my hips, guiding himself into position. I feel him at my entrance, and then he slowly sinks into me. I moan as he fills me.

"That's a good girl," he praises, holding my body against the wall as he slowly begins thrusting in and out of me. I brace myself against the wall, sighing in time with his thrusts.

He kisses the back of my neck and then my bare shoulders. "Fuck, you're so perfect, Ella," he says, pumping harder.

I whimper in response, the pleasure building inside of me. While one hand remains on my hip, steadying me as he roughly pumps away, his other snakes in front of me, between my legs, finding my clit.

I cry out, trying to buck my hips, but I'm at the mercy of Alec. I'm pinned against the wall, unable to do anything but simply take the pleasure he gives me.

"Oh, *god*," I whimper.

"Yeah, sweetheart?" he says.

"*Alec*," I cry, the pressure only building. And finally, I crash over the edge, moaning desperately as my orgasm hits me. Alec comes only a second after me, emptying himself inside of me and then stilling.

We stand there, leaning against the wall, panting, catching our breath.

Alec steps back, leaning down to retrieve my clothes and handing them to me. I smile at him shyly, still awash in the afterglow of my orgasm. I quickly clothe myself, and Alec fixes his pants.

Smiling down at me, he wraps me in his arms, pressing his forehead against mine. "Ella Reed," he says slowly. "Before you start vet school, let me take you on a vacation. A real vacation," he adds when he sees me opening my mouth. "Just you and me. Nothing fake about it."

I bite my lip, grinning up at him. "I could be convinced."

He laughs, throwing his head back. "Oh, that reminds me." He steps back, fumbling in his pocket for something. He finally pulls out what looks to be a small piece of paper. "I have something for you."

I stare at it in confusion.

He holds it out to me, and when I finally recognize it as a check, I shake my head. "You already paid me," I remind him.

"I know." He holds it out farther, and I finally take it. I unfold it and stare down at the sum. I widen my eyes in shock. "What ...?"

"You said a hundred grand would help with vet school but wouldn't fully cover it. Well, I looked up all the vet schools in the area, and that check should cover absolutely everything. Four years, books, you name it."

"Alec, I …" I shake my head.

He closes the distance between us again, pressing a soft kiss to my forehead. "Just take it," he whispers. "No strings, no nothing. Just you getting to follow your dreams."

Joy washes over me while a prickle of tears spring to my eyes. "Thank you," I finally answer.

He leans back to meet my gaze. Then he chuckles, looking away.

"What?" I ask with a giggle.

"Asher and Aiden are going to be so glad I grew a pair and came clean about how I feel," he says, shaking his head.

I laugh. "So are Olivia and Lilly," I add.

He shrugs. "Yeah, the four of them probably saw this coming a whole lot faster than we did."

I nod, grinning. "I'm sure."

"Who would have thought three assholes like us would've landed women this amazing?"

I smack him on the chest. "You're not an asshole."

He shoots me a look.

I shrug. "Well, maybe just a little."

Penelope Ryan

Penelope Ryan writes sizzling hot romances with dominant men and lots of dirty talk and spice.

If you haven't already, be sure to check out the other books in the Billionaire Brothers series, starring Asher and Aiden King. And stay tuned for more spicy billionaire romances in the coming months!

Books by Penelope Ryan:

The Billionaire's Assistant

The Billionaire's Obsession

The Billionaire's Wife

My Best Friend's Billionaire Brother

Tempting the Billionaire

Teacher's Pet

Losing It

The Arrangement

Small Town Billionaire

Did you enjoy the book?

Authors and readers depend on reviews. If you enjoyed the book, please consider leaving a review. Thank you so much!

Printed in Great Britain
by Amazon